DEFY

SIENNA SNOW

CHAPTER ONE

Sophia

*M**URDERER*

People accused me of being many things, but this one definitely sat on a level I never expected to achieve.

Troublemaker, reckless, disgrace, tabloid diva, even whore to the stars based on my most recent media scandal, but a cold-blooded killer, that was a new one.

A shiver ratcheted through my body, and I wrapped my arms around myself as I scooted onto my cot in my jail cell. A tear slipped down my cheek, and I closed my eyes for a brief second before leaning my head back on the cement block wall to look up at the grimy ceiling, which needed a coat of paint or three.

I wasn't sure if it was fear or the rancid stench in the air from whatever fungated around me, but my stomach wanted to upend itself at any moment.

When the cops brought me in, they told me to get comfortable. Was that even possible when someone accused me of a murder I never committed?

Another wave of nausea hit me, and I immediately pushed it down as my eyes caught sight of the toilet in the corner.

I squeezed my arms around me tighter and drew my knees up, burying my face against them.

If I pretended this place was similar to some of the conditions so many other models and I endured during various shoots and fashion shows, I wouldn't have to face the reality of my situation.

Hey, at least I had a toilet in the corner instead of a bucket like the one we used to pee in at the show in Death Valley. If the organizers could cart in facilities for all the A-listers, they could have brought in an extra one or two for the models showing off their designs.

What the hell was wrong with me? Jail and a model shoot weren't even in the same league of comparison.

Closing my eyes, I inhaled a deep breath.

This is what I got for trying to make myself feel better.

I'd made so many dumb decisions over the years. Maybe that was the point of jail, to contemplate all of life's choices, good and bad.

The one thing I never regretted picking was fashion as a career choice. Yeah, it had its ups and downs. At this very moment, I lean toward the down.

But the industry taught me a self-confidence I wouldn't have gained anywhere else.

Then again, maybe my attitude was why someone pinned this murder wrap on me.

I wouldn't lie and say I never wanted Keith Gilbertson Randolph dead.

God, I'd fantasized about it. I'd dreamed of it.

I stared at my hands through a haze of unshed tears, clenching my fists open and shut. I'd created countless scenarios where I'd implemented gruesome acts of torture on that despicable excuse of a fashion designer.

But actually, going through with any of my ideas was impossible.

I wiped away the wetness from my cheeks and then swallowed any remaining tears burning the back of my throat.

I had to get myself together and think clearly.

First of all, I barely made up half of his body mass. There wasn't any way possible for me to take him on, much less the three bodyguards he had with him at all times.

Second, how would I get close enough to kill him when he knew how much I hated his guts?

And lastly, only a loser copied a girl's big brother's signature means of revenge against an enemy. Even though no one could prove it, everyone knew the eldest of my brothers, Lucian Morelli, utilized elimination as a tactic against anyone who garnered his ire.

My methods fell in the range of public embarrassment. So they were illegal but not in any way on par with Big Brother.

A guard walked by, pausing outside of my cell.

I flicked a glance his way, and instead of letting him get a glimpse of the worry and uncertainty coursing inside me, I glared at him. "Do I get my phone call now, or are you still withholding my rights?"

Shit. Why was my voice so hoarse?

"You'll get it in due time, Morelli."

"Due time, my ass. I've been here for three hours. You and your cronies are keeping me from getting counsel."

"Are you so ready to change out of your designer wear and into proper prison gear?"

"What I think is that you had a shady judge sign off on a warrant, and know the minute I meet with counsel, they will have that warrant shoved up your ass."

"You're pretty confident for a woman whose fingerprints are all over the victim's penthouse."

All over? No fucking way. That was impossible.

The queasiness grew in my belly, but I held it together, pushing it back under layer after layer of my smartass side. "Did you check how many other women have their fingerprints all over his penthouse? He likes women and men. Maybe you need to go to detective school again."

He narrowed his gaze. "For a moment, I almost felt sorry for you. My partner believed this beef the DA has with your father and brothers is why you're here. His theory was that he went after you to get back at the rest of the Morellis."

Wait, what? This wasn't about Keith or his murder but about Dad. The DA came after me to stick it to Dad.

My heart sank. Going after me wouldn't make a difference to Dad. In the long list of his children, I ranked at the bottom with Lucian when it came to favorites.

"Let me guess, you've changed your mind."

"I think you may be guilty as charged."

"How can I be guilty when I don't know how

he died?"

He narrowed his eyes and then scoffed as if I was an idiot. "You expect me to believe you don't know what murder weapon was used on the victim? Next, you'll say you don't know when the incident happened."

Oh, I'd figured out when it happened. Keith's demise occurred all while I was busy working behind a sewing machine at a place designed to protect the victims of people like Keith Randolph.

"Might as well fill me in on both since you're accusing me of murder?"

"I'm not accusing you of anything. The DA is the one who pushed for your arrest."

"Whatever. I want my phone call."

"Calling your family won't help you in this situation. Maybe you should call one of your clients the media says you do tricks for in your high-end fashion world. Or that lover of yours. Pierce. He's tied to your brother, from what I hear."

My heartbeat accelerated as I thought of Damon Pierce and the devastation in his green eyes as officers pulled me away from him during my arrest. He'd fought as hard as Lucian to reach me before other police grabbed and restrained him.

Less than twenty-four hours ago, we'd come

together as Damon and Sophia, Dom and submissive. There was no more running for either of us, no more fighting what we felt for the other. He'd claimed me. I was his, and he was mine.

And now this.

"What makes you think I plan to call him?"

Ignoring my question, he continued monologuing, "He's another slick one, a bit more on the straight and narrow. No one heard or seen him do anything illegal, per se, but most of us have our gut feelings. For such a reclusive guy, he sure knows a lot of influential people."

"Is that why you are denying me due process? You're afraid of Damon Pierce and the power he wields?"

"You think too highly of the men in your life. Get comfortable, sweetheart. We'll let you know when it's time for that call."

He walked away without a backward glance.

I clenched my teeth and covered my face with my hands.

What was wrong with me? I allowed myself to walk right into that annoying conversation.

He'd come here to jerk me around.

Fucking asshole.

He wanted a reaction from me, and he got it.

Sophia, do you ever learn?

This was all bullshit mind games.

I knew better. I was a damn Morelli. I needed no one. I could do this on my own.

My lips trembled.

But could I? This wasn't like anything I'd ever encountered before.

A beep sounded on the electronic lock of my cell, and it slid open, making me sit up.

You will not let him see your tears, Sophia. You will not let him get pleasure from your fear. Keep it together.

Taking my internal chant as a bolster to my confidence, I decided if that dickhead came back, it would just let my anger free and deck him. At least then, the dumbasses could charge me with something I'd actually have done. Attempted assault on a police officer was at least believable considering my past actions as opposed to murder.

Who was I kidding? I wasn't going to do shit. I wanted to get out of here, not make it my permanent residence. And with the DA ready to make me pay for something Dad had done to him in the past, there was no hope for any leniency whatsoever.

After a few seconds and no one arrived, the uneasiness weighing on my shoulders grew to an almost unbearable level.

These guys were seriously jerking me around today.

I scooted further up the uncomfortable bed and tucked myself on top of the nearly flat pillow and into the top corner where the two walls of the room joined. From there, I could see every angle of the cell before me.

At least the one good thing about years of never allowing myself to let my guard down was that I could utilize that skill while I was here.

A few officers passed outside my cell with other prisoners. They shot me a quick glance and then moved on.

It felt like being a bird in a cage on display for them.

Shifting my focus, I took in the room around me. Cement blocks made up the walls, with layer upon layer of peeling paint in various shades of blue-gray over it.

I sighed. In the grand scheme of jails, at least I could say, this was a hell of a lot better than the places I'd found myself in during my younger years.

God, I still remembered the hell Lucian had given me when he picked me up from county lockup after I'd spray-painted the words "serial rapist" on the side of the brand-new BMW XM of a prick who'd gotten off on another assault charge because his rich daddy golfed with the right people.

Yeah, I'd only been eighteen then and hadn't mastered avoiding surveillance equipment. When the cops approached me about the incident, I acted like it wasn't a big deal and told them it wouldn't have been an issue if they'd done their job.

It hadn't gone over well with the male officer. However, the female seemed to understand my beef. She convinced her partner to take me into holding for an overnight visit.

The other time I'd spent the night in lockup was after one too many lemon drop martinis. I saw this asshole beat cop harassing a friend of mine for jaywalking. She was only trying to avoid an ex who wouldn't leave her alone, so she crossed the street to avoid him.

Well, the officer couldn't have cared less and was just verbally abusive, so I jumped in and gave him a piece of my mind about manners and how to speak to citizens for better cooperation. He gave less than two shits about my argument, and my girlfriend and I ended up at the precinct. The charges went from jaywalking to underage drinking since we were a month shy of our twenty-first birthdays.

Luckily, Lucian had the charges dropped within two hours, and outside of an ass chewing, a night at his place to sober up, and a good meal, we'd come out of it unscathed.

It impressed me that Lucian kept those antics quiet from everyone, including the press and especially our parents.

I could admit I'd been a bit self-destructive when it came to preserving my reputation. But then again, what reputation was there to keep when Keith Randolph had destroyed it with his lies? He'd turned me into a tabloid sensation.

Yes, I was a well-coveted fashion model with her pick of any show to walk in, and I could decide which campaign I wanted to represent. But I would have given all of it up if I'd had one thing from the very beginning, for Bryant and Sarah Morelli to question the rumors about me that reached their ears.

Instead, they'd believe every one of them before confirming the truth. Not once had they given me the benefit of the doubt, so not once had I given them an inch when it came to presenting myself as the dutiful, conformist daughter as my two older sisters, Eva and

Daphne, had managed to accomplish.

Why couldn't Mom and Dad see that ninety-five percent of what they believed about me wasn't true? All I wanted and needed was for them to take my side just one time.

What the hell was I doing? I couldn't let them fuck with my head in here. I had to keep it together.

The cops were playing mind games with me. I shouldn't do it to myself.

There was no getting around the fact that I'd fucked up when I left my damn fingerprints in Keith's apartment. It gave just enough evidence for probable cause.

But the cop saying "everywhere," that was a damn lie.

Wait. There was no way I could have left any fingerprints.

I traced back through every moment of that stupid night, from the moment Lizzy came to my apartment and demanded she join me in whatever I'd planned for the evening, including the time we spent dressing up as high-end call girls to entering Keith's penthouse to us hiding from security and calling Damon to rescue us.

Not once had I taken my gloves off. Plus, after Keith discovered his destroyed collection and called security, the cops would have dusted every surface of his penthouse for prints. Wouldn't they have come after me then?

I refused to go down for a crime I never committed.

Yes, I vandalized the bastard's designs before Fashion Week, but murdered him?

Hell no. I wasn't guilty.

And on top of everything, no one would tell me how he died. Was he stabbed, shot, run over by a car?

That wasn't the point; I had an alibi—a solid one.

But, if I revealed the truth of my whereabouts, it betrayed my oath to Suzette and the people I protected. I wouldn't betray them. Those women and children had suffered more than enough.

I refused to bring problems to the doors of the shelter.

A chill worked through my body, and I rubbed my hands up and down my arms.

No matter what I did, I was screwed.

"I want my damn phone call," I muttered to myself, knowing full and well there wasn't any hope of getting one any time soon.

"You never know. They may give it to you now that I'm here." A woman with a Russian accent said as she strode in and stopped before me. "I won't bother with my call. I doubt Nikki would help me in any case. He wants me to cool off."

Cocking my head to the side, I took her in.

Beautiful to describe her was an understatement. Tall, almost six foot, by my guess, with long reddish blonde hair worn in waves down her back and golden eyes, reminding me of a tiger.

There was something familiar about her. Was she a buyer for a fashion house or a model? A socialite?

She scrutinized me as intensely as I did her.

She wore a designer outfit that had recently graced one of the runways during Fashion Week. The expression on her face told me coming into this holding area was more an annoyance than worrisome.

That was when I saw the giant rock on her left ring finger. The diamond and its accompanying stones probably ranged in the ten-carat range. Whoever she was, her significant other had fabulous taste in jewelry and the bank account to get her out for whatever she'd done within the next few hours.

"What did you do that you're my roomie for the night?"

"I informed a handsy asshole to keep his body parts to himself on the dance floor of a club." She shrugged. "He didn't like my delivery method of communication."

I followed her glance down at her shoes, which had a few drops of red on them.

For a split second, I could only stare. Then the only thought that came to my mind was, *Oh, I liked her.*

"Let me guess. A knife was involved."

"No, it was an earring. The right pieces of jewelry can double as weapons. I told him to keep his dick off my ass. When he didn't, I pushed it away." She shrugged and then moved to the cot across from me.

To end up in jail for something like that meant the guy was somebody in the upper echelon of NYC.

"Who'd you stab?"

"Nickoli Dominik."

I gaped at her. "You're kidding me. You do realize who he is, don't you?"

He was the head of one of the Russian syndicates that ran a better part of New England.

"No, I'm not kidding. That is what I did. And yes, I know him. Nikki deserved it." She followed up in a string of Russian I couldn't follow, but I assumed they were curses.

I cocked my head to the side, taking her in, and then it dawned on me. She'd said, Nikki.

Holy fuck.

"You're Oliana Dominik." I gaped at her. "You stabbed your own husband?"

What was happening in my life right now? I wasn't sure whether I should cry or freak out. A mob boss's wife was in a cell with me.

"Yes. Nikki pissed me off. He ordered me to give him another baby. I give him five. That is enough." She stomped her foot. "I don't like being pregnant. No more babies."

"So you sliced his balls with your earring in the middle of a club?"

"It's my club. I do what I want."

"How did you end up here?"

She sighed. "Nikki tells me to come here to calm down. He believes I'm nicer once I visit with people here. He thinks if I remember life back home, I will be sweet to him again."

"So you're here by choice."

She nodded. "This is cleaner than where I met Nikki. But it reminds me of where we fell in love."

"I'm not following. You met him in prison." I frowned.

"I was a guard." She grinned. "He's sexy. I help him leave. So when I'm mad at him, I come here to remember."

"It doesn't work that way in the US. They don't arrest you so that you can reminisce about your love life."

"Of course they do. It happens all the time. It is all about who you know and how much money is in your bank account." She shook her head at me as if I was so naïve. "Besides, our people have ways of making things happen when others deny us. Just as you Morellis do."

"You know who I am?"

"Da. I saw you walk the runway in the dress with sapphire and diamond bikini under it. Someone bought it before I could." A flash of annoyance crossed her features before she shrugged. "I'll have her make a custom one for me. Nikki likes emeralds."

"I guess you aren't mad at him anymore if you plan to wear lingerie for him."

"There is no end for Nikki and me unless we go together. Those are the rules."

For a split second, my mind drifted to Damon, his intensity, his possessiveness.

If I ever made it out of here, how were things going to be with us? Would those same rules

Oliana spoke of apply to us?

Instead of letting myself spiral in my thoughts, I asked, "So what happens if one of you breaks the rules? Like if he cheats or you do."

"He knows better." Fire lit her brown eyes. "They sent me to eliminate him in prison, but I didn't. I'm his secret weapon."

A chill slid down my spine as I comprehended what she meant by her words. "You're an assassin who fell in love with her target?"

"Da. It happens. I told you Nikki is sexy. Your man is Damon Pierce?"

Her sudden change of subject and bringing up Damon had my back stiffening.

"Yes. He's my man."

Calling him that felt strange and so right.

What I wouldn't give to feel the comfort of his arms around me right now. He was my safe place.

"He's like my Nikki," she paused, holding my gaze. "And your brothers."

Meaning dangerous. I heard the unspoken words. How many people would tell me this about him?

The rumors about Damon's former submissive had taken their toll on him. She'd taken her own life, and her brother blamed Damon for her death, claiming he'd killed her.

"Being associated with Lucian or his friend doesn't make him so."

"It doesn't make him a simple architect either."

I narrowed my gaze at her. I'd barely met this woman, and in the last ten minutes, she'd blown my mind with her relationship drama. Now, she decided to give me personal advice.

"Okay, I'll bite. What is he then?"

"Let's say, for people like Nikki and others like him, including your eldest brother, Pierce is—"

"Morelli, it's time for that call you want," a booming voice shouted from the other side of the bars of the cell.

My stomach dropped. Of course, now would be the time I'd get my call.

Oliana shooed me with her hands. "Go, I'll see you again soon. And remember to use the underground tunnel connected to the exit on the east side of the precinct. The media forgets about that side of the building."

"Why do I feel you orchestrated our meeting in addition to needing a time out from your Nikki?"

"Because I did. I'll tell you all about it the

next time I see you."

"Is that wise?"

"For you, it is."

CHAPTER TWO

Sophia

"Y OU CAN TAKE your call over there." The female officer directed me to a section with booths and what looked like old-school phones with keypads.

I sat down in a seat, taking in the scent of sweat as well as the pulse of anxiety and worry permeating the air.

To my right, a girl cried into her receiver, telling whoever she was talking to about something not being her fault and that she was sorry and please bring her home.

Somewhere near me, a loud booming roar ordered someone to get them the hell out of there at that very moment, or he'd ring their necks when he got out of there. I refused to turn and identify the owner of that voice.

I made poor choices often enough. Adding more to the mix by pissing off an already irate person by looking at them because of curiosity would do me no good.

Lifting the receiver, I poised my finger over the keypad, ready to dial Lucian's number, but paused before I pressed the first silver digit.

My hand trembled, knowing who I truly wanted to call.

Damon.

He was my safe place. The one I'd picked. My Dom, my protector.

But then again, because of me, he spent the better part of the day treated like a criminal. A team of officers had come into Damon's penthouse acting as if he'd committed Keith's murder and brought him down to the station for hours upon hours of questioning. It had all been a ruse to capture the real target: me.

Before the cops took me into custody, I saw the exhaustion on Damon's face—the dark shadows under his eyes.

I couldn't put the man I loved in more of a precarious situation. My family handled scenarios in this vein without blinking. Whatever Oliana was about to tell me about Damon before we were interrupted meant nothing in this situation.

Calling Lucian over Damon was the right thing to do.

Then why wouldn't the nagging feeling of

guilt evaporate from the pit of my stomach?

Because deep down inside, you want to see Damon above anyone else, Sophia.

Ignoring my inner voice, I dialed Lucian's cell.

He answered on the first ring. "Thank fuck. Those bastards are giving us the run around about bullshit paperwork, overloaded processing system, and other crap. I have a right mind to call in every favor owed to me and have all of them deal with it."

"I don't think having this type of conversation while on the phone with me, especially when I'm in jail, is the best use of our time."

"We're blocked at every turn and haven't had any luck through our normal channels."

I remembered what that asshole cop said about the DA.

"What do you mean? I thought you could get anyone out. Is this DA that powerful?"

"He's only one part of it." Lucian released a frustrated growl. "This situation is a mess. Whoever set you up wants it to stick. And the judge has had it in for us for a while. No one else would have signed off on the warrant with just that one piece of evidence. Fingerprints. There were at least fifty other people's prints in the place. I hate that prick. I hated him when he was a DA, and I fucking despise him even more now."

"Lucian, what does this have to do with bail? There has to be a hearing or something about bail."

"Aren't you listening? The judge is the one who tried Dad for Lane Constantine's murder. That's why he was so happy to lock you up. And with the prosecutor's argument that you're a flight risk because of our family connections to the unsavory elements of the world. He denied bail."

"Are you kidding me? I'm denied bail because of something from our childhood. I'm innocent. You believe me, don't you." I couldn't hide the panic in my voice.

"I know you didn't kill that bastard, no matter how much I wish you had."

"I don't even know how he died. Was he shot?"

"Poisoned."

"Really?"

"Yes."

"Well, that's dumb. Any toxicology test can detect that shit."

"Exactly, that's why I knew you couldn't have done anything that stupid." His deadpan tone had me smiling for a fraction of a second, even though I wanted to cry at the thought of having to move into the actual city lockup system.

All of a sudden I remembered something that happened a few years ago. "Oh God. There's something that I need to tell you. It may have to do with the poison."

"What? Spit it out."

"A model friend of mine made some stupid comment about me using poison to handle Morelli business when I stood her up at a party. It was a dumb offhanded comment."

"Let me guess. It's the same friend you were caught dancing with on a bar top."

"I never was on it. I held her hand while I convinced her to get off the damn bar."

"Shit, Sophia. You need new friends."

I sighed, "I know."

"Why didn't you go? I thought you liked all the parties."

If he only knew how much I hated the parties.

"Keith was on the guest list and so I avoided any place that jackass was going to be at. It was a ticketed event, so I can prove I wasn't at the party and there are text messages on my phone to back me up about what happened."

"I believe you, Sophia."

My throat burned as a small sense of relief washed over me. At least Lucian had faith in me.

"But," he continued. "It gave the fucker who pinned this on you a way to frame you."

"I don't have any idea who hates me this much."

"We will figure it out."

"How did Dad and Mom react?" I regretted asking the question as soon as the words came out of my mouth. "Never mind, don't answer."

It shouldn't matter. I shouldn't care. The little girl in me shouldn't still want the love and protection of my parents when she was scared.

"They are remarkably outraged by the whole situation. Dad more so than Mom."

"Let's be real." I released a sigh. "Mom is more than likely losing her mind about how my arrest and possible future trial will ruin her standing in society. Then she's probably driving Eva nuts with concerns about the drop in headcount for her wedding since guests may not want to associate themselves with the scandal."

Pushing my irritation back, I asked. "Is there any hope of getting me home, or must I accept my fate?"

"You'll handle it for as long as necessary. Is that clear? This isn't long term." The gruffness in Lucian's tone had the back of my throat burning.

He was afraid for me. Lucian never gave away

any of his emotions.

Oh God.

"You make it sound like this judge and prosecutor wants me moved to a state penitentiary instead of city or county."

"That's exactly their plan. They want to make an example of you to get back at our family. It's personal to them."

"I deal with the bitches on the catwalk. Those cunts will cut a girl's face if she gets a job the other wanted and ruin her career. I can handle this."

More pretending. I could do this. I could do this.

Maybe if I said it enough times to myself, I'd believe it.

"Exactly. I'll keep working on my end. Don't think I won't stop."

"I know you won't. Will you call Damon and tell him what's going on?"

"No one's seen or heard from him since they arrested you, and he left the station."

"Does he know about the situation with the bail?"

"I sent him an update, but no response. My best guess is that he has a plan in the works, and he's keeping it close to the chest. Let's hope it works. Fucker is secretive when he is getting things rolling."

"What does that mean?"

"Hey, Morelli. Times up. Back to your evening accommodations." Someone said from behind me.

Turning, I found a burly man with a scowl etched on his face.

As I took him in, I realized he wasn't even looking in my direction. His attention was on something beyond my view.

Okay, that sour face wasn't for me. Good to know.

"Got to go," I muttered.

"Remember, you're a Morelli. Don't take anyone's shit."

"I don't take it from other Morellis. Why would I take it from outsiders?"

"Good to hear."

I hung up and took a few centering breaths. All I had at my defense was the cold mask I'd learned to wear from the time I was a little girl.

I could do this. I wouldn't break.

Squaring my shoulder, I turned to face the cop.

He motioned with his head to follow him, then said under his breath, "Don't these idiots have anything better to do than act as if it's a social hour, standing around to gossip?"

As we made our way down to the cell block where I stayed before, I noticed groups of people kept turning to look my way.

"Why is everyone staring at me?"

"Because you became a celebrity sensation in the past few hours."

"Whatever."

"Nationally and possibly internationally. The media is all over this story, and politicians have started looking into your case."

"Politicians? You've got to be kidding me?"

"The mayor is somehow related to the Randolph family. No one has said anything publicly about that. Still, everyone in the department knows since Daddy Randolph came in puffing his chest about his connections and wanting everyone to throw the book at you."

Well, it wasn't that great.

The officer continued. "Then the Governor called the DA's office wanting information on the investigation. I'm not sure if he is for you or against you. This is over the top, but what do I know."

My shoulders sagged. "This is ridiculous. That's what it is. I didn't kill the idiot. Someone set me up."

Maybe I should want to sit in jail to avoid the spectacle.

No, that was my fear of the press talking. I wanted to go home and hide under my blankets for the next ten years. That sounded like heaven at the moment.

"I'd have to agree. You Morellis are more of the slit your throat or shoot you in the head and dump your body in a landfill or watery grave type. No evidence, no crime type. This is a sloppy job. But since the higher-ups assigned someone else to the case, I'll keep my mouth shut. If the DA and prosecutors want to end up looking like dumb fucks, I'm happy to sit back and watch."

"So you know I'm innocent."

"The law says everyone is innocent until proven guilty."

"You don't seem to hate my family like the other cops do."

"The others act morally superior in one area and turn their head in another. I have no time for those games. Everyone knows your family is part of the ecosystem of the city. They are as necessary to keep things going as the snobby socialites you model your clothes for in fashion shows.

"The way I look at it, as long as your family or

people like them stay off my radar and their business isn't in my line of sight, I don't give a fuck. But once you make it my business, I must do my job. Until then, I don't care one way or the other. Everyone is just another New Yorker walking down the street."

I stopped and looked up at him. "I don't think I have ever said this to a cop. You're a pretty decent guy. I like you."

"From a Morelli, that's high praise." He pointed to a hallway. "Go to the right."

"But my cell is through the doors on the left."

"We aren't going back to the cell."

My heart dropped. The DA was moving me already.

"Where am I going?"

"You'll find out soon enough."

Wherever they took me, I could handle it. Yes, I'd lived a privileged existence. Yes, I'd never wanted for anything. Yes, I was soft in comparison to what so many others had experienced in their lives. But I'd learn to adapt. I'd figure it out.

It would make me stronger.

I remained quiet for the rest of the walk. We took various corners and passageways until I heard commands to put belongings into bags and take uniforms.

"This is where I leave you. You've got this."

I nodded and moved into a giant room with rows of benches and women lined up near each one.

A female corrections officer stepped in front of me. "You Morelli?"

"Yes."

"Take the last space on the fourth row. Change into your uniform." She scanned me from head to toe and shook her head. "Take a sharpie and label every damn item you put in that bag, or you may not see it again. Grab your shoes from the bin on the way to your station."

Following her directions, I picked up my sneakers and moved to my spot.

Before undressing, I labeled everything on the outside of my bag.

"Don't forget your underwear. Make sure you put that down." A sweet voice with a Southern drawl said.

I glanced at a petite woman with red hair and bright blue eyes.

"They want us to take everything off? Even our bras and undies?"

"Yes. It's the rules. Normally, I go to city or county, but since I went too far this time, I'm going to state."

"What do you mean, you went too far?"

She rolled her eyes. "I told my Mack I wanted a night off. I'm his bottom bitch. I deserve a night off after servicing for eight days straight, don't you think?"

"Definitely," I agreed.

"Well, at first, he said, take a break and have the whole weekend. Then he had the nerve to come over with his friends for a birthday celebration." She cocked a hand on her hip and lifted a finger with her other hand. "I negotiate my rates for these situations. And he expected me to perform. Oh, hell no. I put my foot down. That's what I did."

I wasn't sure how to respond to this, so I asked, "Exactly how did you put your foot down?"

"So after I realized they had all come into my place, got naked, and made themselves comfortable in my living room, I pulled out the pistol my big brother gave me when I moved to New York and decided to use it. Slowly I walked in, dropped my robe, let them jerk their cocks, and then shot a ball off each one of them."

"No, you didn't." I couldn't hold in my shock. "Are they dead?"

"Of course not. But that's the charge." She

rolled her eyes. "Five counts of attempted murder, my ass. If I wanted them dead, I'd have brought out the revolver hidden under my bed and aimed directly between their eyes. That gun's got a punch. Ain't no coming back from that one."

I held in my laugh. Maybe being here for so many hours had twisted my mind, but the thought of incarceration wasn't so bad if I met people like her all the time. I could enjoy it.

"I believe you are my new favorite person. You're a serious badass."

"No one has ever said that to me before." Her blue eyes lit up. "I'm Charlotte."

"I'm Sophia." I offered her my hand.

"We all know who you are. People are taking dibs on who can make you cry first. Stick by me. I know most of the chicks in here. I'll make sure no one fucks with you."

She was smaller than me, so I wasn't sure what she could do. But then again, after the story she told me, and considering her line of work, she had to be tough as hell.

"Thanks, I appreciate that more than you know," I said, leaning down to remove my boots. "I better get changed before someone yells at me."

"Good idea. They're looking in our direction."

"Shit." I jerked off my socks and shoved them in my bag.

Just as I unbuttoned my shirt, I heard, "Stop. Morelli, put your shoes back on. They are moving you again."

"Oh fuck," Charlotte said. "That's not good. Did you do something besides off that designer for them to put you in solitary?"

Solitary? I could only stare at Charlotte. Was she for real? Why would they put me there?

I couldn't hide the panic from my voice. "I've been in my cell the whole time. All I've done is call my brother and come here."

"Then the only other thing is interrogation. Remember, the investigators have a habit of acting like they have witnesses. Don't fall for it. They don't know shit. From what I hear, they want your dad, and you are the consolation prize."

"How do you know so much about my case?"

"The whole station is talking about your case. Make sure you follow what I said. Don't let the assholes intimidate you."

I nodded, trying to ignore the acid churning in my gut, slipped on my shoes, and readied to move, but I turned to Charlotte before I shifted. "Thanks for being nice to me. Also, if you get out and you want to leave the trade, I can help you. You can find me through a woman named Suzette Owusu. She's another badass like you. She'll get the message to me. Every other channel wouldn't tell me."

"You may hear from me."

I turned and walked toward the waiting corrections officer.

A few minutes later, we entered a holding area where no one looked in my direction.

"Is this where I wait?" I asked the guard at the door.

"Obviously."

My heartbeat accelerated, unsure of what would happen next.

"Am I going into interrogation? Shouldn't I have my attorney present for this?"

He ignored me, turning his attention to the monitor before him.

A loud beep sounded thirty seconds later, and the white steel door popped open.

"Go through. Head straight to the desk. Don't go anywhere else before you sign the paperwork, or you'll come right back in here."

I wasn't signing jack shit without my attorney present so he could fuck himself with his orders.

"Get moving."

Instead of giving him a piece of my mind, I opened the door and abruptly stopped.

Right on the other side of the guard's desk was the one man I wanted to see above anyone else. Damon's deep, haunting green eyes bore into mine, calling me, stirring all the emotions I'd tried so hard to push down back to life.

My throat burned, and the impulse to run to him, throw myself into his arms, pushed at me. I wanted to feel his touch, to know I was safe.

He clenched his fists as if he felt the same pull. He took a step in my direction but paused.

"He must have deep connections and knows the right people to bribe to get you out of here, Morelli. The way the DA was throwing everything at you, even God above wouldn't have been able to get you out."

I ignored the guard's snide comment but couldn't forget what Oliana or Lucian said about Damon.

Lucian warned me away from him countless times, and I'd refused to listen.

Damon was mine. No matter what he was, I accepted him.

I strode toward the clerk at the desk, who pushed papers in my direction. She pointed to the spots where I needed to sign, never bothering to speak to me.

She huffed when I refused to take the pen she offered and picked up the papers to read them.

If she took me for a dummy, she needed to be corrected.

From the corner of my eyes, I noticed Damon's smirk.

My hands shook when I read the full details of the bail agreement.

On my behalf, Damon agreed to pay fifteen million dollars. I would stay in the Manhattan area until my official arraignment, and under no circumstances was I allowed to leave the country. Damon took responsibility for me, my whereabouts, and all my actions or risked the money offered for my release.

Had he lost his mind?

I turned to him.

"Are you sure you want to do this?"

"Sign the papers," he ordered with a scowl and added.

"What if I don't agree to these terms?"

His eyes narrowed, and I thought of my mom locked under my father's control. Their relationship was its own prison, and now, with this bail, was I signing up for the same thing?

He looked at me like he could read my mind.

"Sign the papers. Come home."

A shiver slid down my spine, and for the first time since before this horrible ordeal began, I allowed the unfettered desire I felt for this man to uncoil deep inside me.

I scrolled my name on the places indicated, and after a few more exit procedures, I was allowed through to the side where Damon waited.

Instead of pulling me into his arms as I expected, he set a hand on my lower back and guided me out.

"Let's go home, My Sophia. We need to have a long chat."

CHAPTER THREE

Damon

I STARED DOWN at Sophia as she squared her shoulders, and we prepared to leave the sign-out room for the precinct lockup. I expected some response to my statement about the two of us having a long chat, but she remained quiet.

Right now it seemed as if she braced herself for a papz to jump out from some corner to take her picture or bombard her with a dozen questions.

Not a fucking chance with me around.

When she'd stepped out from the holding area, she clenched her fists, and irritation marred her features as if she willed herself not to turn around and clock someone.

Then, surprise lit her gaze as our eyes connected. And if I wasn't mistaken, her annoyance switched to longing.

She had no idea how hard it had been not to push past the security barrier and pull her into my arms.

Everything inside me raged at the sheer fact this beautiful creature spent the better part of the last twenty-four hours in this godforsaken place. I couldn't protect Sophia from whatever she'd experienced while they held her.

I'd fucking failed her.

"We will take a more secure route for our exit," I informed Sophia, guiding her toward the precinct's east side. "I don't want anyone knowing you're out before I have you secured at home."

She nodded, her mask still firmly secured over her features. However, I knew this woman. This act was her shield to protect herself so no one saw the vulnerable woman underneath. I knew when she saw that she was being remanded to my custody, she would think of her parents and their relationship and how scared she was to repeat it.

But she couldn't hide the minor telltale signs of relief. Her shoulders were more relaxed, and she eased further into the touch of my hand at the base of her waist.

However, the exhaustion radiating from her tugged at every one of my protective instincts. I wanted to find the DA and punch him for putting my woman through this ordeal.

Using her to carry out personal agendas went

against all the rules in my book. The judge and the DA's office made an enemy of me.

I directed Sophia past another security point, and then an area used more for station staff. Once we reached the east side of the building, we took a narrow hallway and approached the back exit, where two members of my personal protection team came into view. They stood next to my car, with a third holding open the passenger side door for Sophia.

Once both of us were inside the cab of my vehicle and I pulled out of the underground garage, I prepared myself for the questions bound to come from her lips.

How did you get me out? Who did you bribe? Was it Lucian or someone else who pulled the strings?

Except she only stared out the window, head pressed firmly against the headrest.

"Ask, Sophia."

She shifted her attention in my direction. "I'm not following."

"Yes, you are. I know you want to. It's written all over your face. I'd want to know if I were in your position."

"Okay, I'll ask. How did you manage it when no one else could?"

"I called in a favor the mayor owed me."

"That's impossible. He's related to the Randolphs."

"You heard about that connection. Interesting."

"I think the cops thought they could scare me with that information into confessing or something."

"The Randolphs' connections mean jack shit. Especially after I showed the esteemed mayor the video of his dear deceased nephew's exploits."

"Wait. You have Keith assaulting someone on video?" The panic in her voice had me setting her hand on her lap.

"The statute of limitations ran out on that situation a long time ago and the family settled with the Randolphs out of court."

"Another cover-up," she said through clenched teeth.

"Yes. The Randolphs wielded their money and power to hide their son's crimes. I plan to use their son's misdeeds to protect you in any way possible."

"Did you threaten to leak the footage and exploit the mayor's connection to the Randolphs?"

"No. It's more that the mayor now understands distancing himself from certain family connections is better for his political aspirations."

Putting fear in someone's head was good enough. The video's release would only cause the victim to suffer more, and she'd been through enough.

"I don't want you ever to leak it."

"I know, Sophia. I wouldn't do that to her or you."

Her fingers tightened on mine and she grew quiet for a few moments as if lost in thought.

Finally when she spoke, she asked, "And how is the Governor involved in this? Did you call in a favor for a fat donation to his campaign?"

I couldn't help but smile. "That is exactly what I did."

"Let me guess. The favor was my bail."

"Part of it. The other was, releasing you exclusively into my custody."

"Why did you agree to such a high price?"

"I could have gotten a lower amount for the bail, but we all agreed the high price tag would keep the media from thinking I wouldn't put so much money on the line if I planned to help you escape to another country."

She gave a dramatic sigh. "My fantasies of you whisking me off to some tropical place without extradition agreements with the US are shattered.

I was looking forward to laying around in a bikini and having cocktails served under a cabana."

If she only knew how tempted I was to do precisely the very thing she described. But the craving to find out who framed her and put them down was the bigger desire at the moment.

"I don't give two shits about the money. I want you safe, and until I know who killed Randolph, you're always with me."

"You have a job, Damon. I have a job. We can't be together at every hour of every day."

"Want to bet."

"Yes. I have a life outside of you. My commitments include shows, events, photoshoots, and parties."

"I never said you couldn't do any of those things. If you plan to work, attend a show, make an appearance at a party, or even visit a fucking friend, I'm coming with you."

He was out of his damn mind.

I gritted my teeth. "I'm not Maria. I don't need you to control every aspect of my life. That is not how I want to live."

I stared at the road ahead, feeling as if she'd punched me in the gut by bringing up Maria. This was in no way near the same situation as Maria's.

"The last thing I would ever think of you as is Maria."

"You wanting to be with me everywhere is extreme."

"These are extreme circumstances, Sophia. The terms are clear for your release. I am responsible for you, your whereabouts, and what you are doing. And once we get home, I want an accounting of every second of your last seventy-two hours."

"Is this an interrogation, Officer Pierce? That was the one place I never got to see the inside. I'm sure you did. I want to describe it just in case I never get the opportunity."

"Very funny."

"Here is the basic rundown of my not-so-interesting life since the end of Fashion Week. Thursday started at home. I went to my parents, where I received endless lectures on what a disappointment I was to everyone. Then, when I couldn't take the stimulating conversation, I returned home, stayed there all day until I dressed and attended the gala, which turned into an interesting evening, as you know. Since you came in all caveman-like, caused a scene, claimed me. Oh yes, then we had voyeur sex in a greenhouse, went to your place, had more sex, and ended in jail. That sums it up."

"Hardly."

"What did I leave out, all-knowing one?"

I'd never understand why her standoffish attitude turned me on and made me want to choke her with my cock, instead of turning me off as it had done with every other woman before her.

"Plenty."

There were blocks of time when none of my people could verify her whereabouts. And from my sources on the running investigation, this missing piece gave the asshole judge the ammunition added to the fingerprints to sign off on the arrest warrant.

"Want to elaborate?"

"Not at the moment. And for the record, your home is with me from now on."

"I'm not in the mood for this possessive routine."

"Too bad. You knew what you were getting when you let me claim you in the greenhouse. Hell, you all but begged for it. Now, deal with it."

"I don't have to do shit. And I didn't beg. I don't ever beg." She delivered her bratty retort with a yawn, dissolving the intended impact. "God, I'm tired."

"Ten more minutes. Then I'll get you in the

shower and put you to bed."

"I thought you wanted a long talk?"

I wanted a hell of a lot more than a long talk.

"I do, but I doubt you have the stamina for anything besides sleep now."

"I'm tired, not fragile. I can handle anything you have to dish out."

Her annoyance whenever anyone believed she was weak amused the hell out of me. Fiery to the core and an attitude to match.

"My Sophia, the last thing I'd ever describe you as is fragile. I want to take care of you. You've had a long day. We both have."

She'd faired far better than I ever expected. Most women from her world would have fallen apart, not come out looking like they wanted to punch someone. Then again, she wasn't like any woman I'd ever encountered.

Pampered, privileged, princess—most definitely, yes.

Delicate, breakable, flower—not a chance.

We drove in silence for the next few minutes before Sophia said, "I didn't do it."

That came out of nowhere. Of course, Sophia hadn't done it. I doubt she even knew what killed that sick fuck. The Randolphs had gone to a great deal of trouble to keep that part out of the media, just in case they assumed Keith Randolph overdosed on the many substances he was known for taking.

"I never thought otherwise."

"Really? I—never mind." The surprise and then the drift of her words had me glancing in her direction.

Her dark eyes pierced into my soul. So many emotions and so much confusion bombarded me.

Fucking Bryant and Sarah Morelli.

"You will never put me in the same category as your parents."

Fire flashed in her eyes, and then it calmed.

"Sorry. My siblings are the only people who stand by me through everything. This is a new experience for me."

Instead of being loving, nurturing parents and creating a safe haven in their home for their children, Bryant and Sarah fostered an environment of fear and anxiety.

They determined their sons' and daughters' worth based on what each could provide for the family's standing in society.

Sophia had failed them by being different, wanting to shine and be an individual instead of conforming to the mold her mother and father insisted she shape herself into. And because she refused to follow the rules, they threw her away to fend for herself.

Even now, all the patriarch of the Morelli family cared about was how the Judge and DA were using Sophia to get to him, not the fact Sophia suffered because of acts he'd committed in his past. There was no compassion sent in Sophia's direction, no fatherly love or worry.

I'd despised my drunk fuck father, but what Lucian and Sophia dealt with sat on a completely different level of narcissism.

Reaching over, I cupped her cheek and thumbed over her lower lip. "Everything between us is a new experience."

"I'm talking about you believing my innocence without proof, without an explanation."

Pulling my hand back, I focused on the road. "You accepted everything I told you about Maria as the truth. You could have let all the millions of rumors about me cloud your judgment."

No matter how much I wished it, my guilt over the death of my past submissive, Maria, would stay with me for the rest of my life.

I'd never been the right man for her. She wanted not a Dom but a complete power exchange, a Master/slave dynamic, something I'd never consider.

Initially, she accepted my boundaries but then pushed for more, wanting me to meet the slave aspects of her needs and desires. I wasn't the right man for her. No matter how hard I tried to convince her, she believed otherwise.

When her obsession had grown to a level I couldn't handle, I broke things off with her. And then everything spiraled out of control.

"She took her own life. No one murdered her, no matter what her brother said. You were completely innocent. The only reason anyone whispers behind your back is because you never respond to their accusations or defend yourself. You could have prevented all the gossip if you ever bothered to stop blaming yourself for something you were never responsible for in the first place."

"So fierce. Always my champion, even against me. That's beyond anything I have ever had before."

"Better get used to it. I have issues when anyone treats the people in my life badly."

"I could apply the same statement to you."

"It's not the same."

"It damn well is."

"You're impossible." She huffed and folded her arms across her body.

"Pot meet kettle."

"You're a very annoying man. Do you know this?"

"And you're a brat who has a difficult time following directions."

"Oh well, it's too late to back out now since you've put so much money on the line." She air quoted. "You claimed me."

"You enjoy challenging me."

"I enjoy challenging everyone. It's why I've garnered the reputation I have going for me."

"With me, there are consequences."

"Promises. Promises."

"I'm keeping tabs. Remember, I always deliver."

Almost immediately, the energy in the car changed. My body filled with insatiable need for her. I craved to mark her, to fucking possess her, to hear her beg for more as I reddened her beautiful ass.

Her breath grew shallow, and her slight shift in the seat as she pressed her thighs together had my cock growing hard.

"Damon." The breathy way she said my name had me gritting my teeth.

Fuck.

She was too tired for what I planned for her.

"Sleep, Sophia. That's a priority."

First, I'd bathe her and then let her rest. Then I'd get my answers from her, one way or the other.

All I knew was that I'd bask in her beautiful fucking tears.

I honestly was a sick bastard to love her sweet, sweet tears.

"I decide what's a priority for me."

"Can't stop being a brat for even five seconds."

CHAPTER FOUR

Sophia

MY BODY HUMMED as we rode the private elevator up to his penthouse. Well, I guessed it was our penthouse now since he commanded that this was my home now.

Had he meant to shift the conversation to something sexually charged?

Even if he hadn't, my desire for him flared to life with the tiniest spark. His mere presence called to me in a way no other could before.

I shouldn't want to prioritize physical pleasure when sleep pushed at the edges of my consciousness.

Every muscle in my body seemed to ache, and until I'd slipped into my seat, I hadn't realized how exhausted I was from the ordeal of the day. Maybe it was adrenaline or sheer will that had kept me going. Now, my tank barely ran on fumes.

The need for a bath to clean the grime of the

day screamed at me, but that seemed like too much damn effort.

"Do I have to shower?" I dropped my head against Damon's shoulder. "Throw me in the guest bedroom so I don't dirty your sheets, and I'll freshen up in the morning. I'm so tired."

"First of all, you smell like a jail cell. A shower is not optional. Second, you and I sleep in the same bed. That's how this works. Third, I know you're tired. I'll do all the work, and you go along for the ride. Then I'll tuck you in for the night."

"What about the long chat?"

"You can barely keep your head up."

The elevator dinged, and the doors opened. Just as I took a step to exit, Damon grabbed my arm, pulled me against him, and leaned down.

"And before we have our discussion. I plan to fuck the hell out of your bratty, little cunt."

My heartbeat jumped, and an ache grew between my legs.

"It's unfair to tease when you don't plan to deliver."

"I never said I played fair, Ms. Morelli."

He held onto my waist as we moved into the penthouse, down through the living room, and toward the primary bedroom.

Damon turned on the shower and then removed each piece of clothing from my body with slow, gentle movements.

It was as if he inspected every inch of my skin as he went, ensuring himself that nothing happened to me in jail. When he had me naked, he walked behind me and scanned my back.

"I hated that you spent one second in that place. None of those bastards deserved a second of your presence."

I turned to look at him. His emerald eyes burned into mine. There before me were the same emotions I saw the moments before my arrest.

"I don't know how to respond when you say things like that."

"Say you're mine."

I set my hand on his chest. "I'm yours."

I wanted to say more. It burned inside me to say it. I couldn't risk pushing him, scaring him away if it was too much for him.

"Time to clean up." He pulled open the glass panel for the giant shower. "Step inside. I'll be there in a few moments."

"Are you sure that's such a good idea?"

He smiled. "Have no doubt I want to lose myself in that body of yours. However, I can resist my urges no matter how much you beg me."

"You think I'm going to beg you to fuck me?"

"I know you will."

"You're pretty sure of yourself."

"When it comes to your sexual craving, I'm an expert."

"I can't argue with that. Then you know what I want."

"I also know what you need, which is care. Once you've rested, we can revisit this discussion."

His words sent a shiver down my spine.

"You're doing this on purpose." I glared at him and moved into the shower, stepping straight into the multitude of shower heads spraying in various directions.

I braced my hands on the tiled wall, letting the water pour over me.

"God, this feels like heaven," I couldn't help but groan as the heat seeped into my skin.

Was it only forty-eight hours ago I'd walked into a gala with high-end call girl scandal finally simmering down and no thought of a future for Damon and me?

Man, how things change.

I should have expected the world to turn on its axis when Damon made that very public scene at the gala, letting everyone with eyesight know I was his.

And then the craziness with his former submissive's brother when he decided to crash the party and accuse Damon of murder hadn't made anything easier.

Was this murder charge God's way of telling me I wasn't deserving of happiness?

I shook the thought away. That was my mother crawling into my head.

A sadness hit me.

That seemed the only place she'd reach out to me.

The clang of the glass door had me turning and blinking water out of my eyes. Once my vision cleared, I nearly swallowed my tongue.

Damon stood before me, completely naked. A work of art, better than most of the models I encountered in my work.

I love his defined arms and shoulders. When wrapped around me, I was safe.

The rest of him wasn't any less appealing. A broad chest with a light dusting of hair and a firm stomach with a "V" leading to a cock that I'd thought was way too big to fit the first time we'd had sex.

I'd given him my virginity in every form possible.

"Stop looking at me like that. Turn around.

I'm here to bathe you."

"I can manage."

"It's my job, Sophia. I take care of you." He moved closer, his naked body brushing mine, sending goose bumps over my heated skin.

Arousal pooled between my legs, a warning sign this shower would play havoc with my exhausted mind and body.

No matter how much I wished otherwise, I craved this man's touches, caresses, kisses, and presence.

Being here, depending on him, I knew was dangerous. There was so much we didn't know about the other. So many secrets, so many untold stories.

"Stop thinking so hard. You are in no condition to solve any of the problems running through that head of yours. Turn around and let me tend to you."

He set a hand on my waist and shifted me to face the wall. Water cascaded over us, pelting our bodies and steaming the enclosure.

He dropped a kiss to my shoulder and took my wrists in his hand, the feel of his arms around me giving me the comfort I should want so desperately.

Tears pooled in my eyes. He was my safe

place, where the world couldn't get to me, at least for now.

In all the times things fell apart, this was the first time someone was there to help me pick up the pieces.

Damon brought my palms flat against the tile, caging me with his large mass. "Rest them here. Let me do all the work."

"You pose your words as if they are a request." I cocked my head to the side, watching as tiny droplets of water slid from the tip of his nose. "But I know it's an order."

"I am who I am, My Sophia. Now be a good girl, and let me clean you up."

"If it makes you feel like you've accomplished something with your life to give me a bath, go right ahead."

He narrowed his gaze. "We'll add that one to the list, too."

"What list?"

"The list of your infractions requiring punishment." The slight change in his voice had my core spasming.

"What infractions?"

"Let's start with you questioning whether or not I wanted to pay your bail."

"Oh."

"Exactly, oh. You will never question your worth with me. I would have gladly paid triple that." He poured shampoo into his hand. "We'll discuss the rest tomorrow. Tilt your head back."

He washed my hair in a way that shouldn't have felt so seductive. It was a scalp massage. I reacted as if they were fingers strumming my clit. He found all the right spots to release the tension from the day, and I couldn't quite understand why the simple act of him washing my hair dialed up my desire so much.

I nearly groaned with disappointment when he angled the shower head to wash away the suds. However, my angst disappeared when I realized he still had my body to focus on.

He lathered a loofah with earthy scented soap, not flowery, more with a hint of botanical herbs. It soothed the senses.

He washed my skin in slow, leisurely strokes, followed by the glide of his hands to massage my muscles.

I couldn't help but moan at the exquisite touch. It was both soothing and arousing. Damon circled my breasts in what seemed more of a tease, as if he wanted my nipples to strain into tight buds before he moved lower down my abdomen.

"You're doing this on purpose."

"Doing what?"

"Torturing me."

"If I wanted to torture you, I'd do this." His fingers delved between my folds, stroking along the sides of my clit, giving it the barest of grazes but not enough friction to give me the edge of pleasure I craved.

I pushed against the tiled wall of the shower, bringing my back flush to his very aroused front.

"Damon, make me come."

He slid free of my sex. "Tsk. Tsk. Orders don't work on me."

Taking the soapy sponge, he knelt and ministered to my lower body. His movements were deliberate, meant to arouse and increase the throbbing ache deep in my core.

The way he tended to my feet had shivers prickling all over my skin, not from a tickling sensation but from how much this simple act increased the desire coursing through me.

When he finally reached my desperate pussy, I thought I'd collapse from the prolonged wait. His palm glided between my legs, soapy suds teasing my clit.

I arched into his touch, lifting one hand to cup the back of his neck.

"Put that hand back." His command held a

bite I hadn't expected.

Following his order, I stood straight again, some of my desire fleeting.

I had to remember this wasn't about sex but him tending to me. The fact his touch aroused me was my own body's self-inflicted torment.

Asshole had turned me into a sex addict for his cock.

Keeping my attention on the wall, I ignored the pleasurable feel of his hands as he finished bathing me and waited for him to turn off the shower.

Instead, he crowded me toward the wall.

"Isn't the shower over?" I asked.

He wrapped an arm around my waist and drew me to him, the press of thick, hard cock a brand along my ass.

"Not yet. I have one thing left to do."

"I know you aren't going to make me come, so just put me to bed and let me sleep."

My mood had grown cranky from the mix of exhaustion and unquenched arousal.

"I said I wasn't going to fuck you. I never said I wouldn't make you come."

"Yes, you did."

"Did I?"

"Damon. Please, don't tease me."

"Did I just hear you beg?"

Shit. Was that begging?

"Absolutely not. My words were a request."

"Such a liar." His hands came up my belly and between my breasts to up my throat to clasp around my neck in that way I loved oh so much.

He squeezed, and my breath grew shallow, and my pussy contracted.

My head lulled against his shoulders as my breast swelled and my nipples tightened into stiff peaks.

Fuck, I wanted to come, I needed to come.

Fine, I'd admit to begging if he'd only let me come.

"Did you say something?"

Had I spoken aloud, or was he reading my thoughts?

"Make me fucking come, Damon."

"Listen, Brat. You come because I let you come. I will leave you hanging as I've done before. Do you need a reminder?"

I needed no reminder.

That day in the club, Damon had fucked me like an animal, drove my need to a blindingly painful level, and then the bastard held me there, refusing to let me go over while he continued to pound into me at a pace meant only to allow him to come.

I'd spend the next week in agony, desperate for release. On top of everything, it was in the middle of Fashion Week, so projected the cranky model stigma to a 'T.'"

"Asshole. I will take care of it myself then," I shot back.

"I'd like to see you try. We both know the only way this cunt of yours"—with his other hand, he parted my fold, stroking back and forth—"will ever find satisfaction is if I administer the orgasm."

"You think too highly of yourself."

He thrust three fingers into my pussy, making my back bow.

"Your hand, your toys, nothing will make you come like I can." He pumped in and out in a rhythm meant to push me to the edge but not send me over. "I've ruined you for self-administered satisfaction."

"Bastard."

"Even so. It's still the truth."

"I admit to nothing."

"Of course not. However, it doesn't change the facts."

"What facts?" I lifted my hips to meet his fingers' demands, wanting so much more.

"Your sweet virgin cunt was all mine. I popped that cherry. I popped all your cherries. My cock branded every part of you. Your pleasure comes at my command."

He scissored his digits inside me to prove his point, causing a delicious sting. My breath grew shallow, and how he held my neck drove my arousal higher and higher.

My pussy quivered as it flooded his hand with my desire, then spasms shot through me, followed by hard contractions. Just as I reached the precipice of what I craved, he withdrew.

"No, I hate you."

"Do you?"

"No, I don't hate you."

He gripped my waist and scraped his teeth along the back of my shoulder, hard enough to sting without breaking the skin. "Tell me you can find this same thing with someone else."

He had to be kidding. There wasn't anyone like Damon Pierce. From the moment our eyes connected across Lucian's club, I was lost.

He'd seduced me with one look and turned my world upside down. His touch, his taste, his sheer presence. There was no one else like him.

Releasing my throat, he walked us backward until we reached a stone bench. He pulled me astride him as he sat, my back to his front. He splayed wide apart, setting them over each of his, exposing my swollen, aching pussy completely.

His thick, long, beautiful erection bobbed underneath me, a heavy presence, telling me how aroused he was. Heavy beads of precum dripped from the tip, and my pussy contracted at the sight.

Damon fisted my hair, jerking my head and bringing my attention to his face. At the same time, he thrust deep and hard back into me, curving his fingers, rubbing along the bundle of nerves so sensitive I could barely breathe when he touched them.

I bucked and rolled my hips, lost in the torrent of pleasure pushing to the surface.

My nails scored his forearms as I bit my bottom lip and clenched my eyes tight.

"I should hate you for making me feel the way you do."

"But you don't."

"No. I don't. I'm desperate. Don't make me wait."

"What is it that you feel, Sophia?"

He knew. It was in my eyes when they brought him out of the holding area after they took him in for questioning. I was sure I'd revealed even before that.

The jackass crawled into a space I'd promised never to let any man occupy.

Now, I was in love with a man with as many demons as I carried.

Opening my lids, I stared up into his mesmerizing emerald eyes.

I wanted to give him the words, but some part of me told me to wait until things weren't so volatile, until I no longer had a murder charge hanging over my head, until our relationship wasn't so fresh and untested.

And most of all, what if he never felt the same way about me?

I knew he wanted me. He was more than possessive over me. I had no doubt he cared for me beyond anyone before me. Could I risk hearing he didn't feel the same way?

"That isn't for tonight. Not now. Not here."

"I know you feel it."

"Even if I do. I won't say it. It's too soon."

His hold on my hair tightened.

Before he could respond, I pulled his mouth down for a kiss and then murmured, "Please just make me come. I'm going to die."

"I'll let you win this one for now," he murmured against my lips.

A sense of relief washed through me, knowing this subject was no longer on the table.

Damon's thumb circled my clitoral nub. A whimper escaped my lips, and the constant spark of heat deep inside my core ignited into a painful, raging fire. My pussy clenched and flexed as his hands worked me, driving me higher and higher.

He cupped my breast, squeezing and molding, taking the nipple and pinching hard, giving me the bite of pain I loved so much.

I gasped, "Yes, more. Just like that."

I slide closer and closer to oblivion.

"That's is. Come for me. Let me hear you scream." He pulled out of my pussy and then slid two fingers along the sides of my clit and pinched it between his knuckles.

That was all it took. The pleasure-filled pain exploded through me, and ecstasy cascaded into every nerve in my body. My body bowed, and I could do nothing but let Damon hold me as I thrashed and let my orgasm roll from one wave to another. It felt unending, euphoric, and something only attainable with this man who held me.

CHAPTER FIVE

Damon

"DON'T YOU WANT me to take care of that?" Sophia asked as I toweled her body dry, and she focused on my ramrod cock.

Of course, I'd love nothing more than for her to wrap her lips around my dick so I could force her to take me to the back of her throat.

Hell, all I'd wanted to do was mark every damn part of her inside and out with my cum from the second she let me claim her in that greenhouse two nights ago. The primal urge pushed at me even more after the last twenty-four hours.

She was mine, and some dared even to think to harm her, to take her from me.

"What happened in the shower was for you. I'll get mine soon enough."

I hadn't intended for the shower to become sexual. Still, I realized using the powerful pull Sophia I had for each other would take her mind off the shit show she'd endured.

Somehow, this woman, even without trying, seemed to turn what I meant as something focused on our mutual, unexplainable physical desire into something emotional.

A rage churned inside me that only she could calm. She had to know it. It drove me to find the fucking bastards who set her up and destroy them, piece by motherfucking piece.

She stayed my hands as they slid up her hips. "What if I want to give you relief?"

A yawn escaped a second after her question, and I shook my head.

"You are asleep on your feet. I need you wide awake for what I have in store for you."

No matter how much I gorged on her, I wasn't sure I'd ever get enough.

But I sure as fuck, planned to get those words she refused to give me. I wanted those words. I needed those words. They belonged to me.

"Oh, I remember. You plan to punish me. Whatever." She followed her retort with a half-assed frown, which lessened the impact of her brattiness.

I stood and picked up a hairbrush. "Let's finish up in here. You look like an exhausted kitten, needing me to tuck you in for the night."

"I have a pussy. I'm willing to let you service it again."

Instead of continuing a nonsensical conversation, I combed and dried her hair and slipped her into our bed.

Just as I was about to tell her not to argue and sleep, I realized her eyes were closed, and she had already passed out into a deep slumber. Tucking the covers around her, I turned down the lights and exited the bedroom.

I'd barely come down the hall when I heard the ringtone of my cell phone. I'd left it on the kitchen island intentionally, knowing someone or the other would call.

By now, the news of Sophia's departure from the station was public information, and either the media or her family would expect updates.

Avoiding the media wasn't the problem. Her family was where the issues came in, especially Lucian.

Fucker probably wanted to cut my balls off for keeping him in the dark about my plans.

When I reached the mobile, the call dropped, and the alert for my private elevator sounded.

Good thing I had it on lockdown.

No one besides me could override that system.

As I reviewed the display on my mobile, I

released a deep breath and prepared for an inquisition.

As I'd expected. The devil was on a rampage and at my doorstep.

I had fifteen missed calls from Lucian and at least fifty messages, each text becoming more profanity-filled as they progressed.

So, deductive reasoning told me that my lobby guest was the one and only Lucian Morelli.

I glanced in the direction of the hallway leading to my bedroom. The distance and soundproofing of the penthouse would keep any noise brother dearest graced me with from disturbing Sophia's rest.

The last thing I wanted was for anyone, including Lucian, to upset her. I wanted her as relaxed as possible to answer my questions in the morning.

I was a sick fuck, but my way came with pleasure mixed in with the torture I planned.

Deciding not to make the dickhead wait more, even if annoying him added some fun to a shitty day, I punched in the code to allow access to the lift.

Less than four minutes later, an irate Lucian stormed through the front entrance of the penthouse and into my living room.

"Where is she? I want to see her." Lucian's dark eyes blazed as if he was ready for war.

He stalked toward me, and if I were anyone else, the look on his face would have made me piss in my pants.

However, since I was among the few people the fucker couldn't intimidate, I tucked a hand into my pocket and leaned an elbow against the floor-to-ceiling window overlooking the city.

After letting him stew for a second, I responded, "You'll have to wait until morning."

"The hell, I'll wait." He prowled in my direction, clenching his fists. "Get her out here now."

"She's sleeping," was all I said, and then I shifted and strolled to my wet bar.

"Get her up. I want to see if she is okay with my own eyes."

I pour a glass of soda for me and a finger of whisky for Lucian.

I never drank. I never acquired a taste for it or desired it. Having a sick fuck alcoholic of a father who abused his wife and children too much while under the influence could do that to a person. But who was I to keep others from their preferred choice of beverage as long as they indulged responsibly?

Plus, this jackass was the only one who came

here anyway, so his preferred drink was the one I kept in stock.

Bringing the glass to him, I said. "I'm not waking Sophia up, so fuck off with your demands. I don't give a shit who you are."

"She needs to be with her family."

I was her fucking family now.

"Exactly, where would that be?" I glared at him. "You mean at your parents' house? A place where your mother can degrade her and blame her for ruining your sainted sister's wedding. And your father can pretend she is the reason for all the misfortune in the family instead of the fact a vendetta against him put her in jail?"

"I'll take her to my place. She will be safe there."

"No, she stays here. With me."

"She's my sister. You don't have any claim over her."

That statement had me smirking, which immediately got his back up. "Is that so?"

He knew damn well what kind of relationship I had with Sophia.

"Don't fucking use her."

"I will punch you in the face if you say that again. Why did you send her to the greenhouse if you believed that bullshit about me?"

"You're keeping me from her."

"I am responsible for her. Sophia needs rest. That is the priority over your peace of mind."

"I should put a bullet in your head."

"It's your prerogative. Then you'll have to find a new facilities director for clean-up projects and disposal."

"Everyone is replaceable. Accidents happen all the time."

"Hmm. A lot of murders happen around the Morellis. No wonder they want to make an example out of Sophia." I clenched my fingers around the tumbler in my hand. "This whole thing is a sloppy mess."

"What do you know? And how did you get her out?"

"I know she's innocent." I glared at him. "And I know a dumbass did the job and decided to frame her."

"Well, that leaves me out." Lucian's bland tone eased some of my irritation with him. "Though we wouldn't be in this situation if I had done it. I wouldn't leave a body behind for anyone to find."

"Since I'm part of your clean-up crew, I wish you had done the deed."

"You aren't part of anyone's crew. You're

useful only when you want to step in." Anger radiated from Lucian. "You should have handled Randolph the right way from the beginning. This is what happens when you decide to warn a motherfucker instead of removing them from the scenario."

"The nuclear option isn't always the best."

"In this case, it was."

"The priority is to find out who framed Sophia, not ruminate about the past."

"I don't care who you are, don't put her in more danger."

"My methods aren't yours."

"It's just as dirty, even if it doesn't spill actual blood." His dark gaze bore into mine, an unsaid rage radiating toward me.

Then it hit me. This was all about me leaving him in the dark about the strings I'd pulled to get Sophia out. He felt as if this put him in my debt.

Fuck that shit.

"This isn't about keeping a tally of favors, jackass."

His face hardened. "Did I say it was? You need to keep me informed."

"Oh, did I hurt your feelings by not bringing you in on my plans?"

"She's my sister. I have a right to know the

terms for her bail."

"The terms are very simple. I am responsible for every aspect of her life, twenty-four hours a day, from where she goes, what she does, and who she sees."

Anger flared in Lucian's eyes. "What the hell are you playing at, Pierce? This sounds like what Maria wanted from you, and now you plan to force it on Sophia."

"I'm not forcing anything on Sophia. She's my woman, and I will do whatever it takes to keep her safe."

"She's been through enough over the years."

"Still warning me off?"

"No, that ship sailed. Sophia is a grown woman and made her choice."

"Then why the warning?"

"Because I know how you are and the way Sophia will react. You'll only get to push this one hundred percent control thing so far. She doesn't do well with anyone being too overbearing or possessive. She'll eventually push back and rebel. That's when the true test will come."

His words felt like an omen, and something deep in my gut grew unsettled as if I knew I couldn't hold onto her.

I'd die before I let anyone take her from me.

"Advice noted."

"How much was bail? I'll cut you a check."

"That's my business. Sophia is mine to protect." I held his gaze. "Her bills are mine."

"It's like that is it?"

"It is."

Lucian knew more about me than anyone else. He had my back through everything. I'd do the same for him. However, when it came to Sophia, she came before everything else.

Yes, she was his sister, but didn't hold a candle to what Sophia was to me. She was my first priority. Just as I expected, Lucian's wife Elaine and his children came before everyone else to him.

Lucian pulled a checkbook from his pocket, opening it to reveal Bryant Morelli's name. "Let the old man cover the cost. It's his fault the mess happened anyway."

"Still forging Papa's signature?"

"I brought this as a formality. In the modern world, all I have to do is wire transfer it."

"Let him keep it. I have a feeling, in the future, he's going to need all of his cash."

I'd hand that man over on a silver platter if it meant Sophia was left alone.

"What were the terms of her release?"

"She is in my custody at all times. I claim

responsibility for all of her actions."

"You legally put her in a fucking cage."

"Don't make me use the gun you threaten to shoot me with, Morelli. I'm protecting her until I find out who framed her. Someone wanted Randolph dead and used her as a scapegoat."

"Let me guess, you plan to utilize every resource available to find the real killer."

"Naturally. And I'll call on yours when necessary."

"Is that an order?"

"Hell would freeze over the day you took orders from me."

"As long as we understand each other."

I sat on my couch, not bothering to tell Lucian to join me. He'd do whatever the fuck he wanted, and that was usually the opposite of anything I suggested.

"Randolph's list of enemies is vast. How do you plan to narrow down the suspects?"

"The best place to start is with the list of his former and current business associates. He has a reputation for double-crossing his partners. Those with money already on the line have more at stake than those he insulted or smeared in the press."

"You're saying it's a crime of passion."

"Obviously, with the use of poison. And it

also means it's someone who had close proximity to him."

"Poison? Who the fuck uses poison nowadays? Toxicology can trace that shit."

The outrage in Lucian's tone echoed my sentiments when I'd heard about the method used to off Randolph.

"Exactly. No one brought up in your family would consider such a sloppy means of eliminating an enemy. The DA's ego is running this case, and I want to play into it and let him get lax with the investigation."

"What I want to know is that if they found Sophia's prints in the fucker's penthouse, why didn't they find Lizzy's?"

"That's a question I've wondered about too. Something isn't adding up. Sophia and Lizzy wore gloves when I picked them up the night of their renegade incident. There was no way she left fingerprints at the scene."

"I knew she was too smart for that shit. She's a Morelli, after all."

"Be a proud big brother when we aren't trying to get her out of a murder wrap."

"Jackass." Lucian took the armchair across from me, pulled out his phone, sent a text, and then stared me in the eyes. "Someone planted her fingerprints and that someone knew about her visit to Randolph's penthouse that night."

"That leaves anyone from her fellow vigilantes to those at Randolph's apartment when he discovered his destroyed designs. It was well known the people he surrounded himself with weren't loyal to him, only to his bank account."

"What are you planning to do?"

"Keep her from the predators of the world. What you and your family have never done?"

"What the fuck do you mean by that?" Lucian shifted forward as if to punch me.

"You didn't protect her from a piece of shit like Randolph."

He clenched his fist. "I didn't know anything about Sophia's assault. She kept it from us."

"It was your job to watch out for her. She was eighteen fucking years old, working as a model. It was your damn responsibility to keep her safe. Where was her security? Did anyone bother to find out the truth about what was happening in her life?"

It infuriated me to think how she'd coped with life after Randolph cornered her, assaulted her, and then set up a tabloid scandal to keep her quiet, essentially destroying her reputation.

Sophia had survived it all on her own. There

was no one she could rely on to protect her from the horrible things spread about her. Her own parents hadn't supported her.

And I knew firsthand what this idiot was up to at the time. He'd been so wrapped up in his selfish lifestyle to pause for even a moment to give a shit about Sophia.

"I can't change the past."

"No, you can't, but I will ensure she has a future."

Lucian stood. "You feel that strongly about the situation, then I'm taking it as a vow, Pierce. Don't break her heart, or I will take great pleasure in killing you."

"I don't need your treats. And it would help if you remembered Sophia is the one who chose me. I warned her away. I ordered her way. But just like you, she's hardheaded and doesn't listen to a damn thing anyone says."

CHAPTER SIX

Sophia

I STIRRED FROM a heavy sleep, my body feeling as if it were engulfed in a warm, safe cocoon. I refused to open my eyes and face whatever the day had waiting for me. The bedroom still lay cast in darkness, so it could be four in the morning or the afternoon, for all I knew.

The exhaustion I'd felt when Damon put me to bed no longer plagued me, but the weariness of knowing this whole mess with Keith's death wasn't going to end any time soon sat heavy in my chest.

Nothing made sense.

It just wasn't possible for me to leave my fingerprints in Keith's apartment. I wasn't that reckless.

I was reckless, but when I went on my escapades, I made sure never to leave traces to lead back to me. Fingerprints and hair were major parts of it. The cap holding in my hair beneath the wig ensured not a single strand of hair would escape, so when had I taken off my gloves to leave a damn fingerprint?

I hadn't. Some fucker set me up. But why? What had I ever done to anyone for them to hate me that much?

God, this was giving me a headache.

I'd rather have woken up to an orgasm instead of this mess.

A small ache filled my heart.

It seemed as if every time Damon and I took a step forward, something forced us to take ten back.

This time, it wasn't him with the accusations of murder but me.

I guessed this made us the perfect pair.

Releasing a deep sigh, I opened my lids, knowing it was time to face the day ahead and leave the warmth of this bed.

Instead, I found myself caged in by two strong arms and piercing green eyes staring down at me.

"Hi." I shifted my hands to realize they were bound to the top of the bed, making my heartbeat skip a beat. "Is this how you expect to have that long chat you planned?"

"Not quite."

"Damon."

"Sophia." The way he said my name shot straight to my core.

It was as if a simple change in tone worked as the ignition switch to my libido. A prickling sensation burned along my skin.

The slide of his thick cock along my body as he'd tugged the covers off me told me he was as naked as I was.

How long had he waited for me to wake up? How long had he watched me pour through my thoughts and worries?

"Right now, you and I are the only people who belong in this bed. Is that clear?"

"I don't know what the hell you're talking about."

"Then I better help you figure it out."

I gasped as he placed something freezing cold at the top of my chest.

Ice.

Immediately, a burning sensation penetrated my hot skin. Drips of water slid between my breasts, and I arched up, back bowing.

In the next second, the torture device disappeared.

"Why did you do that?" I glared at him.

"Because I wanted your attention on me, on what I planned for you. You are no longer Sophia

Morelli. You are my submissive."

Understanding dawned on me, and arousal hummed throughout my blood.

There were no murder accusations, no troubles, no dramas.

Damon and I were the only things that mattered.

He ran his tongue along the seams of my lips before nipping the bottom one. I couldn't help but moan and lift up, wanting more.

"Do you want to play, My Sophia?" The rich rasp of his voice had a flutter running deep in my belly.

I nodded, unable to look away from his mesmerizing emerald irises. "Y-yes."

"Are you ready for what I have planned for you?"

"If I say yes, will you fuck me at the end of the scene?"

His lips curved, and my heart skipped a beat. This man who rarely smiled was absolutely devastatingly breathtaking when he did.

It felt as if with only me, he showed this side.

"Wouldn't you rather I fuck you during the scene, brat?"

A flood of desire pooled in my core, and my nipples beaded as my breasts swelled.

"I'm greedy. I want both."

"Of course you do." He reached over to his side, brought out a black silk mask, and slipped it over my eyes.

My senses fired to life. I hadn't noticed the sound of instrumental music and a light floral scent earlier. Or the soft, cool sheets touched my skin in a sharp contrast to the heat of Damon's body braced above me.

It was as if he created a vortex around me, a heady presence that cocooned and protected me. In this space, I could let go.

Damon settled his palms along the base of my throat, where lingering moisture remained from the ice. With lulling strokes of his hands, he massaged down the column of my neck and shoulders, moving slowly lower and lower.

"If a massage is part of a scene. I'm all for it."

"This is to prepare you for what I have planned next." He kissed my navel and rubbed his stubble above my pubic bone, causing goose bumps to prickle my skin. "You're going to love and hate it."

"I trust you," I said without thinking.

I spoke nothing but the truth. With my body, I knew Damon wouldn't hurt me. He wouldn't betray me. He'd push me but never cross the line.

My heart was what I questioned.

"I'm glad. Now we begin."

The bed shifted, and I heard the clang of ice right before his mouth grazed my breasts, his lips cooler than usual, telling me he held a frozen instrument of torture between his teeth.

Now I understood what he meant by love and hate.

I held my breath, expecting the burning cold sensation, but couldn't help but gasp the second it touched my breast. My nipples puckered as Damon rolled the cube around them, straining toward him, and my core contracted at the dueling feel of hot and cold.

Then I released a guttural cry from the back of my throat and jerked on my restraints as burning fire engulfed one nipple and just as fast stemmed.

"Oh dear God, what the hell was that." Tears pooled against the mask covering my eyes, and I could barely breathe, only able to inhale shallow pants.

This wasn't what I wanted, or was it?

"First, tell me if you liked it and want more." Damon's fingers glided along my pussy lips, stroking my sopping cleft. "Your cunt is telling me a lot, why don't you."

I swallowed, not understanding whether or not I enjoyed the white-hot pain I'd just experienced.

This extraordinary need ignited, pushing at parts of me I never knew existed. It was as if the pain released a delicious hormone, shooting it through my blood and making me crave more. I had to have more.

"I—I loved it. Do it again."

"Are you sure?" He crooned in the wicked way of his that teased and warned. "I won't lead with ice after a few more drops."

"Drops?"

"Yes, drops from candle wax. That's what you experienced. Without the ice, it will become intense. Are you sure you can handle it?"

A scene flashed in my mind, one I saw at Lucian's club, Violent Delights. The couple performed a wax play scene on stage. The Domme covered every part of her submissive's body, including his penis, in wax, and he loved every second of the experience. It was beautiful and turned me on more than I realized.

This was long before I met Damon, long before our eyes connected, and everything changed for me.

Now, it was my turn to experience it.

Swallowing, I nodded and said, "I'm sure. I want this."

That was all the permission I needed to give him. Damon's mouth encircled my other nipple until my nerves froze. Then fire burned through me, clouding my mind as it warred with the dueling burning sensations.

He played the game of ice and melted wax all over my breasts for, I wasn't sure how long. I relished every moment of the tingling, the pleasure-filled pain, the endorphins shooting through my body.

I was more than ready when he no longer used the ice and trailed hot, molten wax along my arms and legs.

I squirmed to get away and begged for him never to stop. I loved every moment of it.

My core clenched with every splash. I thrashed and jerked against the restraints, holding my arms as I grew desperate for the orgasm only Damon could give me.

"You said you'd fuck me. What are you waiting for?" I tried to close my legs, needing to relieve the ache, but he sat between them, making me suffer.

"I still have plans. You aren't ready yet."

I growled, "Are you kidding me? I'm ready.

I'm so ready."

"I have to clean you up first, then I'll consider using my cock."

"You evil bastard."

"Every time you call me a name, I will remind you that you picked me." He pulled my legs wide apart, setting a thigh over each of his, and then he lay his thick, rigid cock along the swollen folds of my sex. "You are so ready for me. I bet the second I slide into this sweet cunt of yours, you'd come all over me."

A spasm rocked through my pussy. "Please, just do it."

"Are you begging, Sophia?"

Immediately, I stopped moving and then blew out a frustrated breath.

"No, I don't beg. That's a fucking demand."

He moved forward, spreading me further apart and rocking his hips back and forth, making sure to rub the head of his cock against my aching clit with each pass.

All it would take was a slight shift; he would be in me, and I'd find oblivion.

"You're in no place to make demands." He braced a hand on either side of my head. "Let's get rid of all the wax first. Then we'll consider where to put my cock."

"Asshole."

He rolled his hips, tormenting my swollen clit, driving me closer to madness. "True enough. But that's what you like about me."

Before I could return with a retort, I gritted my teeth and then moaned when he worked the first bit of wax from my nipples.

"Oh."

I hadn't expected the suction and slide of it to feel good.

"Like that did you?"

"Yes. Do it again."

"Sophia, Sophia, Sophia. Never stop giving orders or being a brat. What am I going to do with you."

A fist squeezed my heart, and for a brief second, I almost wanted to say, "Love me, not just protect me."

But instead, I said, "Make me come."

"Eventually." He tugged the wax from the tip of the other breast.

I arched toward him, feeling as if the tingle in my nipples was connected directly to my clit.

I never believed it possible, but this man could get me to come from just playing with my nipples.

"You had to have done something to my skin

during the massage to make it feel so damn good now."

"Correct. The way I see it, clean up can be just as enjoyable as making the mess."

"You have mad skills in the bedroom, Damon Pierce."

"Complimenting me isn't going to get you fucked faster." He removed another piece of wax from my cleavage.

This felt good, but nothing like the way it had on my nipples.

"It was worth a shot."

"You are unlike any Morelli I have ever met."

"I'm well aware of this."

"It's a good thing. You will never get lost in a crowd."

"I'm just another Italian girl rebelling against her family. Nothing new."

"I'd find you anywhere, even blindfolded." He shifted, and the movement caused his hard cock to press harder against me.

Through gritted teeth, I muttered, "That's because you're an obsessive, possessive psychopath."

"Since your cunt is currently weeping all over this psycho's cock and begging for me to fill it, I'd say you're just fine with it. Now, stay still. Almost finished."

"I am the Morelli known for making questionable decisions." I tilted my pelvis, hoping for a fraction of relief, but he held me down and tugged more of the wax off my body.

"I'm the choice you can never take back."

"You're insane."

"A second ago, I was a psychopath. Which one is it? Am I insane or a psycho?" He came over my body.

His weight now settled so much firmer against me. His thick cock pushed against my desperate pussy, making me hungry.

"I'm the insane one. I will lose my mind if you don't fuck me soon."

"Psychopath it is." He bit down on the mound of one breast, giving it a delicious sting, followed by licks and grazes of his teeth.

He gave the same ministration to the other side. All the while, his engorged erection lay thick and heavy between the lips of my sex.

Every time he moved, he rubbed along my slickness, a calculated torture meant to heighten my arousal and drive me closer and closer to the edge.

He was evil and wicked and oh so wonderful.

I tugged on my restraints, and my pussy wept,

desperate to be filled.

"You're soaking these sheets. Was I right? Did you love and hate it?"

"Yes," I answered, knowing there was no point hiding the truth. "I want more."

"You're very greedy, Sophia Morelli." He nipped my ear.

This man understood my body better than I could. He gave me the means to explore things I never permitted myself to open the doors to before him.

He'd never push me beyond what I could handle, and if we ever skated the edge, I had my safeword. I knew he'd stop the moment it spilled from my lips.

I doubted I'd ever utter the word with him.

Marriage.

A tingle shot down my spine.

Once upon a time, that word brought so much anxiety into my mind. The thought of it meant chains, restrictions, abuse.

I wasn't sure anymore. Maybe with the right—nope, I wasn't going there.

Get that thought right out of your head, Sophia.

"What's wrong?" Damon brought his face close to mine. His breath coasted over my lips.

"What makes you believe anything is wrong?"

"I can read every single reaction of your body."

"You think you have me that figured out."

The next thing I knew, he slid the mask from my eyes, flooding them with light.

As my vision adjusted and his deep green irises came into focus, my heartbeat kicked up a beat.

"I know I have." The hand settled between my breasts, glided upward, and cupped my throat. "Now, what were you thinking about?"

"Us."

His fingers tightened, making my breath quicken.

He leaned down and licked the stray tears running along my cheeks.

Why he loved when I cried, I'd never understand.

"What about us?"

"Our future."

"Let's get this straight. I'm not letting you go anywhere." The intensity of his response had a flood of desire pooling between my swollen pussy lips.

"Y-you can't keep me unless I want to stay, Damon." My heartbeat accelerated as his green eyes darkened, and the torrent of emotions I saw overwhelmed me.

We held gazes as he crawled down my body until his face was below my belly button. "You won't want to leave."

"You're very cocky, Mr. Pierce." I gasped as he blew on my sensitive clit and then grazed it with the tip of his tongue.

"If nothing else, you'll stay for my sexual expertise." He parted my folds and took a long swipe that had me bucking my hips off the bed. "We both know I've ruined you for anyone and everyone else."

"As if you'd let anyone touch me."

"Psychopath, remember? You're mine, Sophia. And this cunt, is forever exclusively mine." His mouth descended on me, and all coherent thoughts evaporated from my mind.

He feasted on me, circling my clit and thrusting his tongue deep into my pussy. Unhurried, he licked, sucked, and tasted, pushing me closer to that edge I desperately needed to crash over.

It was an exasperating and wonderful agony.

I exploded on his tongue the second he pushed two fingers into me. My pussy contracted and flexed around his pistoning fingers, and my mind and body cried in relief for the orgasm that seemed so out of reach only moments earlier.

Tears streamed from my eyes, and I flew from

one wave to the next as he continued to work me with his mouth and hand.

I'd barely come down from my third ride over the cliff when Damon thrust his stiff, engorged cock deep inside me.

Instantaneously, my pussy quivered as pleasure-filled pain rocketed through it, and my weaning arousal ignited into a raging need.

He reached over me, releasing my hands, massaging them as he brought them down.

A feral light entered his eyes, and my desire ratcheted up a notch.

"Are we about to have that long chat of ours?" I asked, knowing his mind was on anything but talking.

He pulled out and slammed back in. "I rather fuck you insane."

"I can live with that."

He covered my mouth with his, setting a relentless pace. His thrusts hit all the right places, pushing me closer and closer to another orgasm, one I knew would be more mind-blowing than the last.

He pinched and worried my nipples as he pounded harder and harder into me, then cupped my throat. The firm presence of his hold shot a wicked shiver down my spine. It was everything I wanted and more, unyielding and intoxicating.

"Say it. I want to hear you say it."

So did I, but I wouldn't get them.

"No. It isn't the time."

"Dammit, I want the words."

"You'll get them when I'm ready."

His thrusts grew erratic, and his cock grew thicker and harder inside me. He clenched his teeth and then rolled his hips in that perfect way, and I detonated, clamping down on his pumping cock.

Immediately, he began to come. We both screamed our releases.

Just as he worked the last of his cum out of him, he muttered, "Always the fucking brat. I hope you know I wouldn't have you any other way."

Good, because he was the only one who believed it wasn't a bad thing.

CHAPTER SEVEN

Sophia

"GET ON YOUR knees, Sarah. It's time for you to perform."

"Not tonight, please. The children are home. They will hear. They will know."

"You're panting like a bitch in heat. You want this."

"I don't. I do this for you."

"That's right. And when you please me, I reward you. Now get on your knees and suck his cock while I fuck you."

The buzzing of Damon's phone and the bed shifting snapped me awake.

I blinked a few times and focused on the silhouette of Damon as he moved out of the bedroom with his mobile against his head.

What time was it? I blinked a few times, trying to clear the haze of my dream and focus on the now.

Was it a matter of hours since I left the precinct or days?

Stretching my arms above my head, I moaned. The only aches lingering in my body were from the marathon rounds of sex, not the ordeal I'd faced from the time I'd spent in city lockup.

Damon understood that I needed to forget the reality of my life and lose myself in us, the pleasure, the pain, the desire.

I never believed passion existed on a level like the one I shared with Damon. It scared me.

What if I lost myself in it?

What if he used it against me?

What if I became like Mom?

No, I wouldn't soil what I had with Damon by putting it in any category as my parents.

A flash of the dream appeared from moments earlier in my mind. I was in my childhood bedroom, next to the library, hearing the activities of my parents.

I remembered flashes of things from long ago. I knew some of it may never make sense since I viewed it from the lens of a child. But I now understood others entirely, making me despise Bryant Morelli with a passion to rival my brothers.

And then Mom, a victim, but not at the same

time. She took the abuse for the privileges.

Everything about my parents revolved around preserving what they actually loved—power, money, status. And they would go to any lengths to keep all of them, even if it meant destroying their children. They had to know I could hear them. Why would they want me to listen to them?

Still, that dream about my childhood haunted me. They came in higher frequency now. I wasn't sure why.

Maybe it was the increased stress in my life, and my mind wanted to remember the events of my past.

Honestly, I hoped I never remembered. I had more than enough trauma to deal with at the moment. If my psyche decided to block something from my childhood, more power to her.

Whatever happened in that library needed to stay in that library. Those demons needed to remain locked away.

Rolling from the bed, I strode to the bathroom to freshen up with a scalding shower.

Less than fifteen minutes later, I entered Damon's closet with one towel wrapped around my wet hair and another tucked around my body.

"What to wear?" I asked myself, tapping my

lips.

Until I moved my things from my apartment to this place, my selection of clothing was limited to whatever I could manage to fit me from Damon's wardrobe. The man's body mass was more than double, probably triple that of mine, and with his height alone, his shirts would come down to my knees, looking more like dresses than anything else.

Hmmm. That gave me an idea.

I pulled a deep blue button-down shirt and coordinating tie from a rack. I found some tie pins after a quick search through a few drawers. Then, with a few adjustments to the fasteners and the rolls of the sleeves, I slipped on the shirt.

Next, I fastened the buttons and cinched in the waist with the tie.

Moving to the full-length mirror in Damon's closet, I studied my creation.

It still needed something. Returning to the closet, I grabbed one of Damon's belts and brought it to the mirror. Sliding the tie off my waist, I wrapped it around Damon's belt and then clasped it around me.

"Not bad, if I do say so, myself."

I shifted from side to side. Accessorized with the right jewels and a pair of black stilettos, I could see this outfit on a celebrity as they walked the red carpet at the premiere of a movie or show.

Mental Note: remember this outfit idea.

God, I loved fashion.

Giving myself one last look, I returned to the bathroom, set my hair into a slick knot at the top of my head, and exited the bedroom.

Halfway down the hallway, my stomach grumbled so loudly it could have doubled as a roll of thunder. At least my appetite was back. I hadn't eaten anything of substance since before the ordeal with the police began.

At least something in my life decided to return to normal. One thing I never shied away from was food. As a model, it also meant I had to work out five times as hard.

Hey, I was an Italian girl who liked her pasta. I would rather eat and then have to hit the gym than deprive myself of the pleasures in life.

Though, I'd heard a rumbling or two from a few designers who commented about my ass.

Those were the dickheads whose jobs I turned down. Then again, I knew I was lucky to have the ability to turn them down.

Just as I reached the archway leading into the breakfast area, I heard the rumble of Damon's voice. He sounded irritated and ready to give someone a verbal smackdown.

"I told you to have the information to me hours ago. No, that isn't an excuse. Find out everything about them. Their financials, their partners, every one of their hopes and dreams."

Moving into the room, I saw him pacing back and forth, pausing every so often to look out the window at the skyline of New York City.

"Obviously, the family has enemies. Everyone knows this. I want all you can get on them, too." He ran a frustrated hand through his hair. "No, this is not an option. I'll work on my end. You work on yours. I don't want any holes."

He hung up, dropping his phone on the breakfast table overlooking the city. He braced both hands on the back of a chair for a few seconds as if lost in thought with the worries of the world on his shoulder.

Then all of a sudden, he lifted his head, cocking it to the side a fraction.

A tingle slid down my spine.

"Eavesdropping isn't polite."

"It's not eavesdropping if I came in search of sustenance and you were occupying the space where I can procure my desires."

He turned to face me, his green gaze darkening as he took me in from head to toe and back again. "Procure your desires. What exactly are those desires?"

"Food."

"Are those the only desires?"

I liked my lips. "At this moment, yes."

"I see." He slowly strolled in my direction. "That shirt looks familiar."

He stopped in front of me and thumbed my collar.

"It should. It once belonged to you."

"Once?" He lifted a brow. "Does that mean it doesn't anymore?"

"I've customized it for other purposes. It may be the first piece in a collection I plan to design."

His mouth curved up at the corners, and he took hold of the open collar of my makeshift dress and traced it down to the top swell of my breasts and then over to where his tie pins attached at various points along the sides.

"Your talents are far and wide, Sophia Morelli."

"Are you trying to flatter me into letting you get into my pants?"

"You aren't wearing any pants." His hand skimmed up my knee and between my thighs to stroke my naked pussy.

Before I realized what he intended, he pushed

two fingers inside my slick sex, scissoring them to give me that bite of pain and then curving to rub against the sensitive area deep inside me.

I clasped onto his shoulders, trying not to lose balance.

"Do I ever need an excuse to get between your legs?"

He gave me shallow thrusts meant to tease and incite. I dug my nails into his firm muscles. So lost in the exquisite heat building in my blood.

"As your Dom, do I need any other reason than the fact I claimed this cunt to do whatever I want with it, whenever it pleases me?"

He pumped harder, making it so he held me up as my legs could no longer hold my own weight.

"I don't hear an answer."

"No," I gasped. "You don't need an excuse. You claimed every part of me to do with as you please."

"That's right." His thumb and forefinger grasped my clit, tugging and rolling it in that perfect way.

Immediately, I fell over the cliff. My vaginal walls contracted and then clenched in a rhythmic dance around his wicked fingers.

I dropped my head to his chest, completely

lost in the pleasure this man coaxed out of me within seconds.

I couldn't understand why his possessiveness, his demands, his dark, haunted nature pulled at something so primal deep inside me. I wanted to fight it and revel in it at the same time.

This thing with him made absolutely no sense.

We'd only begun this relationship, and my attachment to him went beyond anything I wanted with any man.

As my orgasm weaned, Damon slid from my body and brought his hands to my lips.

"Suck."

Lifting my lashes, I held his gaze and wrapped my lips around his fingers. My essence exploded over my tongue, a salty, sweet taste I'd learned to enjoy because of him.

His pupils dilated as he withdrew from my mouth, gripped my jaw, and then covered my mouth with his.

The kiss was brutal, consuming, intoxicating, something I could lose myself in for hours.

I couldn't help but whimper when he pulled back.

"It's time for that long chat."

"You want to chat with my brain all sex-addled?"

"I never intended to addle anything. But now that you mention it. Your predicament may help me get clearer answers since you won't have time to dodge the questions."

"Your sexual prowess is top-notch, Mr. Pierce. However, I need food, or those euphoric hormones swimming in my blood will disappear, and all your work will be for naught."

"Then I better feed you." He moved to the oven, opened it, pulled out a prepared tray, and set it on the counter.

Then he went to the refrigerator and gathered containers with prepared salads.

"You had food delivered?"

"No. I rarely, if ever, get takeout." He glanced over his shoulder.

"You like to cook?"

"Why is that surprising? I enjoy my privacy. Therefore, I learned to cook."

"And so, while I slept, you decided to make me dinner."

"I made us dinner. It's nothing fancy. Chicken with a white wine sauce and sautéed vegetables with a salad on the side."

White wine sauce? Okay, that wasn't fancy.

I smiled at him. "Thank you."

"You're welcome."

Over the next fifteen minutes, we filled our plates, sat in the breakfast nook, and ate in relative silence. It was comfortable, relaxed, without the need for unnecessary conversation.

With anyone else, long periods of quiet would have me questioning whether or not something was wrong. Damon made it easy just to be me.

Once we cleaned up from dinner, I leaned against the island and said, "I supposed you've been patient enough. I'll let you off the hook. Let me have the inquisition."

He smirked, approached me, and then caged me with his arms.

"It's you who's impatient for the questioning, Sophia. I can wait as long as necessary. Part of the fun is making you wonder what I plan to ask you."

"Oh, so you're fucking with my mind, am I correct?"

"I'm your Dom. My whole role is to fuck your mind before I ever come close to fucking your body."

My core clenched, and arousal pooled between my legs.

"We are discussing two completely different scenarios."

He leaned forward. "Are we?"

"What is it that you want to know, Damon? I know it has nothing to do with you being my Dom."

"You're mine, my submissive, my woman, mine to protect, to keep safe. So it has everything to do with being your Dom."

"Ask your question."

He grasped my jaw, and his green eyes bore into mine, making my heartbeat accelerate at an abnormal speed. "I want to know if you left your apartment the night Randolph died."

"My building security verified that I stayed in my apartment all night."

"That's not what I'm asking you, and you know it."

He had to have found out some discrepancy about my alibi. Oh God, I couldn't tell him the truth. I'd made a vow, which was the only way to keep those women and children safe.

Wait. I'd worn a disguise. I always wore disguises when I left my building and took the back exit, never the main one used by the tenants.

Was he having me watched?

"Do you have people spying on me?"

"I wish that was something I thought of sooner."

His answer made me frown.

"It would also put you in the category of stalker since we weren't together then."

"Assholes like Randolph wouldn't be able to get to you, so I don't see a problem with it."

"But ones like you could."

He shrugged. "You'd deal with it. Now answer the damn question. Where were you between the hours of five and eleven the night Randolph died?"

Swelling down the bile that rose in my throat, I looked him in the eyes and gave him the truth, but in a way, he wouldn't believe me, "I can't tell you what I was doing, but it wasn't killing Randolph."

"Dammit, Sophia. Where were you that night?"

"According to building security, I was in my apartment."

Guilt settled heavily in my gut.

I could evade and let lies spill from my lips without remorse with anyone else, even Lucian, but with Damon, it felt so wrong.

He'd shared so many truths with me, and here I was, playing this game and skirting around the truth.

"And according to you?"

"I can't tell you."

His face grew hard. "Sophia, two separate camera feeds on two different buildings caught a woman in a red wig with a remarkable resemblance to you leaving and returning to your building at those precise times."

"It could be a coincidence."

"Sophia, I know it was you." His face was a hairsbreadth from mine. "I saw the images. I am intimately familiar with your body and know every curve."

"Perhaps you're mistaken."

"No, I'm not. And the way you're having the hardest time holding my gaze says I'm not."

"It says nothing."

"I can't protect you if you don't give me all the information. Where did you go, and what did you do?" He pushed me against the island with his large body. "And before you lie to me, don't think I haven't noticed how you have skirted doing just that with evasions. I'm not one of those idiots at the station. Just like your brother, I'm a breed of my own. You've only seen certain parts of me. Lying to me is a mistake."

"I haven't lied to you."

"You haven't given me the truth either."

"I don't have to do anything I don't want to

do."

"Someone pinned a murder on you. You had gloves on when I picked you and Lizzy up that night. They planted your fingerprints in Randolph's penthouse. We can't figure out who pinned this murder on you if you don't tell me where you went."

"I can't, Damon."

"Or you won't?"

"Both."

"I'm ordering you to tell me as your Dom."

I gaped at him. He couldn't be serious.

Before I could respond, I continued, "That's what you signed up for, remember? Tell me what I want to know, or deal with the consequences. And for the record, the severity of your punishment is high considering the list of infractions I've collected."

"I'll take the consequences. At least, it will clear this list of yours and give me a clean slate."

He stepped back, gripped my waist, turned me, and settled his palm between my shoulder blades, pushing me down onto the cold stone of the island. "Don't say I didn't warn you."

CHAPTER EIGHT
Damon

I STARED AT Sophia's back, frustration riding me, as well as the need to punish her for defying me at every turn.

All I wanted, all I asked of her, was a simple fucking answer.

Where was she the night some fucker poisoned Randolph?

If she gave me the information, I could use it to narrow down the bastards who framed her. Someone knew she wasn't home. Someone had access to her fingerprints.

It had to be someone with access to both her and Randolph.

But of course, Sophia refused to cooperate no matter what the situation. What was she protecting? Who was she protecting?

She wouldn't have gone on another of her vigilante missions, knowing the trouble she encountered the last time she decided on such an idiotic escapade.

"I hope you're ready for what I have planned."

She glanced over her shoulder with a scowl. "I can take anything you dish out."

"Why won't you trust me with this one secret? Do you have any clue what I'd do if anything happened to you?"

I opened up to her, gave her parts of me I never showed a soul, and she held back.

The glare on her face morphed into what I could only assume was regret. "I—I can't."

I closed my eyes, calming myself, allowing my irritation to slip to the back of my mind.

Maybe the best course of action was to walk away, deny her my touch. She'd grown addicted to me and the way I made her feel. She craved it. If I withdrew my attention, then she would cave to my demands. The way she'd begged me to fuck her in the shower last night was proof enough.

However, my intent to deny her my touch disappeared the moment I opened my lids.

Sophia's beautiful ass shifted side to side in the dress she designed from one of my shirts. The fact she used my clothes and my things to create the masterpiece she wore filled me with a desire to possess her.

My reactions to her made no sense. Nothing

with her made any sense.

Right now, I needed her tears, her whimpers, her torment.

I lifted the hem of the shirt to cup her round ass and found her bare underneath. And if I wasn't mistaken, wet as well.

Last night, I gave her a mix of pleasure and pain to soothe her, giving her the oblivion she needed to forget her worries.

At this moment, there were no orgasms in her future. I wanted her as frustrated as I was. Because then she might tell me what I needed to know.

The punishment I planned would only leave me somewhat satisfied. But it would have to do.

"We will see." I reached around her waist and unbuckled the belt she used to bind my shirt to her body.

The second I pulled the leather free, the cotton flared out, inching higher over her ass and exposing her long muscular legs.

I unwound the tie wrapped around the belt and reached over Sophia's body. Taking her arms, I positioned them above her head, stretching them as far as they could go, and then bound them.

"You will keep your hands here at all times, no matter what I do."

"Whatever."

"Sophia. You asked for this."

"I did."

Then, I took the side of the belt without the buckle and slid it between her knees, gliding it up to her exposed cunt and down again.

Her breath immediately grew shallow, coming out in tiny pants, and her fingers flexed where they rested on the granite.

On my second pass, I rubbed the edge of the belt along the seam of her pussy lips. She shifted and squirmed as slick arousal coated the expensive leather.

"You get so wet, My Sophia. Are you anticipating pleasure at the end of this?" Moving back along her inner thigh, I coated her skin with her essence. "Do you think I'll fuck you into ecstasy after I finish administering your pain?"

"I know there is no repeat of last night." She shook her head. "Stop teasing me and do whatever you're planning."

"Haven't you learned? I enjoy teasing you. I take great pleasure in keeping you anticipating what's to come. I love taking you to the edge."

I dragged the belt up and down four more times, and with each pass, I focused on stroking her clit back and forth, arousing her and making her more uncomfortable.

She pressed her thighs together, trapping the belt between them. "Damon, just punish me and get it over with."

"Do you know what I plan to use as punishment?" I jerked the strap free and coiled it around my fist.

"You're going to whip me with the belt."

"I think you're anticipating it more than worried about it."

"It will still hurt. Isn't that the objective?"

"That's only part of it." I took the belt and positioned it on her back. "The other part involves depriving you of something only I can give you. I have a twofold punishment for you."

Then I moved in behind her, pushing down my lounge pants, letting my cock spring free. Taking it into my fist, I pumped up and down before positioning myself at her soaked opening.

She growled as realization dawned on her.

"You wouldn't do that to me again," she muttered through clenched teeth.

"Wouldn't I?" Instead of pushing into her, I skimmed the head of my dick through her slit, stopping at her clit, circling it, and then moving to her weeping center. "You hold out on me. I sure as hell can hold out on something you want."

She tried to push back into me, but I held her

still with my body, refusing to give her any control. Today, her body was mine to use, to tease, to torment.

"It's not the same thing, and you know it."

"You're right. What you want is an orgasm." Fisting the bun holding her hair, I jerked her head back. "What I want is information to protect you. Not the same thing at all. One more chance to tell me the truth. Where were you the night that bastard died?"

"I can't tell y—" I slammed into her before she could finish her sentence, making the belt drop to the floor.

She screamed at the impact of my invasion, her beautiful cunt immediately flexing around me.

Shoving her forward, I pulled out and thrust in hard enough to make her come onto her tiptoes.

"Oh God."

"God has nothing to do with this. It's Oh, Damon." I pulled out and drove back in, gripping her waist and giving her no leverage to touch her feet to the floor.

I wanted her helpless and at my mercy.

She liked it when I was brute with her when I was rough. It got her to that edge of release faster, to the point of coming, to the second right before her cunt squeezed the hell out of me.

Tears flowed from her eyes, and I loved every microscopic second of it.

The woman was beyond beautiful, and when she cried. I wanted to lick every part of her. It wasn't her model's good looks but the inner essence of her—a unique innocence wrapped in a package of confidence and rebellion.

I pounded into her, feeling my release building and my balls drawing up. Filling her with my cum was a pleasure, unlike anything I'd ever experienced. It marked her as mine.

Until her, I never went bare, and now there was no other way.

I'd continue to fill her with every drop I could until she gave me something I never wanted with anyone else. But first, I had to get her to see it wasn't a trap.

A hard spasm pulsed around me, bringing my focus back to Sophia.

Oh, hell no, she was not getting hers. I wanted her to suffer and ache until I decided she deserved her pleasure.

Her muscles continued to quiver around me, and she whimpered as I adjusted my pace.

A sick part of me reveled in the tears spilling from her eyes. "Damon, don't do this."

"Consequences," I gritted out, unable to do anything but let go.

I held her immobile. Her hips pressed flush against the counter as hard, hot spurts of cum filled her.

I owned this pussy, and she would damn well understand it. She muttered curses at me as the last of my release emptied out of me, and I couldn't help but smile.

Until Sophia, never had a woman fucking made me talk or smile during a scene or sex. I'd done everything possible to avoid women like her—submissives with a bratty side.

With her, I couldn't get enough, and for some reason, I crave the challenge.

Well, except for when she put her safety on the line.

I pulled out of her, giving her no room to adjust except to set her feet on the ground.

Panting shallow breaths, she glared at me over her shoulder, her hands still stretched across the island. The blaze in her eyes was hot enough to set a house on fire.

Yet the tears streaking down her face made her more alluring and reduced the effect she may have garnered with anyone else.

Ignoring her ire, I pulled up my pants and

reached for the belt. "Now count to ten."

"Why am I counting?"

"Don't you want the rest of your punishment?"

"Not really." She dropped her head down onto the stone, resignation in her tone. "Fine. I'll take it. Anything is better than this limbo you left me in."

"The pain associated with a belt is far worse than deprivation of an orgasm."

Instead of responding, she turned her face away from me and flexed her fingers into fists.

"Let me remind you. You chose this." I folded and took the belt into my hand, positioning it to sting but not cause damage. "Count."

Lifting my arm, I brought it down on her round ass.

Smack.

"Fuck," she gasped, then whispered, "O-one."

Immediately, my cock jumped, reawakening at the sight of the reddening mark on her golden skin.

Smack.

"Two."

Smack.

"Dammit, that hurt." She glared over her shoulder.

"I guess we will act like that one never happened since you missed counting it."

"Three. That was three."

"Too late. Missed opportunity."

She muttered, "Asshole," under her breath, and I couldn't help but shake my head.

"Would you like to start over?"

"No, no. Sorry. Keep going."

"Would you like to tell me the truth about where you were that night?"

Smack.

"Four."

"Sophia," I warned.

"Okay, okay. Three."

That was when my cum slid out of her and down the inside of her leg. She squirmed, feeling the heat of it, and the flush on her cheeks deepened.

The urge to fuck her senseless and forget about my agenda rode me. No matter how many times I lost myself in Sophia's body, it never was enough.

"You wanted that to happen," she accused.

"It wasn't intentional, but I can't say I'm disappointed."

I collected the mixture of our combined climaxes from the inside of her thigh. I brought it back to the juncture of her pussy, circling it around her clitoral nub.

"Seeing my cum mark your pussy is a pleasure I savor."

Sophia pushed against my hand as I worked her sensitive bundle of nerves. "This is evil."

Abruptly, I stopped and stepped back. "Yes, it is."

"You're being cruel."

"I am. Now keep counting." I continued the delicious torment on her voluptuous ass.

By the time she called out ten, she was anticipating the bite of the belt, lifting into each stroke.

And the way her hot, hot tears soaked her face mixed with the glow on the skin along her thighs and ass was like having a living, walking dream in front of me.

Her cunt poured with arousal and need. With the slightest graze, she'd detonate. However, this was her punishment, and no relief lay in her near future.

"Damon, please. I'm dying."

"No, you're not." I tugged the shirt down and then helped her to stand.

I steadied her with my arm as she gained her bearings and her eyes cleared of the haze of lust, torment, and frustration.

I fucking loved every minute of this. Sophia was so beautiful and completely at my mercy.

"I hate you for doing this to me."

"Who was the one that decided to suffer the consequences?" I lifted her into my arms. "And I know with certainty that you don't hate me."

"Are you so sure?"

"Absolutely. Tell me, Sophia."

She dropped her head against my shoulder. "I can't tell you. I wish I could."

"No, it's that you won't."

"I'm sorry, Damon."

"I'm not. You deserved your punishment. Just remember, I'll hold back as much as you do."

"I have reasons for what I do. I promise it isn't to hurt you."

"Ditto. You won't win this one, Sophia. Someone is after you, and I will burn this world down and lock you in this penthouse before I let anyone hurt you."

CHAPTER NINE

Sophia

"You attended the fashion show. I consider that more than enough suffering for one evening. You can sit in the car and wait for me while I go into the club. I know this isn't your scene."

"You're my scene. I go where you go." Damon set a hand on my lower back as we made it past the valet stand. "Did you forget the terms for bail?"

"The terms state, you are responsible for me and my actions or whatever. I'm not going to start a fire or a fight. Give me a break."

"You're stuck with me, end of discussion."

Ignoring my glare, he ushered me through the VIP entrance of Milo, the nightclub hosting the after-party for the fashion show we had just attended.

The club belonged to the wife of the fashion designer who premiered his new collection. Since the location was within a block from the fashion school where the show took place, it made it very convenient for celebrities and A-listers to drop in for a photo-op.

The second I cleared security, a multitude of eyes shifted in my direction. The heavy weight of their scrutiny felt as if a barrel of bricks bombarded my head.

Sensing my unease, Damon's fingers flexed on the exposed skin at the back of my dress, and then he said, "Take a deep breath. I'm here right by your side."

His words grounded me more than I wanted to admit, and the comfort I felt from the heat of his palm lessened my irritation from the scrutiny directed at me by so many people who recognized me.

They sized me up, trying to see if there were any signs of trauma from the ordeal I'd faced over the last few days or if I'd give them anything to gossip about behind my back.

Assholes, all of them.

Well, maybe not all of them, but most.

Drawing on my debutante training, I held my emotionless mask in place. I made sure not a single soul saw any kink in my armor.

After all, my goal for tonight's endeavor was,

first and foremost, to establish Morellis never faltered, and nothing phased us, not arrests, not personal vendettas, or murder accusations. Life ran as usual in our world, no matter what anyone threw our way.

I selected everything on my body, from my outfit, and meticulously applied makeup to my hairstyle for impact.

With my signature black diamond earrings and a black diamond necklace Damon had surprised me with right before we left, I knew I oozed understated wealth and elegance.

I'd perfected this illusion long ago, and at this moment, I used it as a shield.

Reaching up, I stroked the pendant between my breasts and quickly pulled back my hand.

No wasted movements, Sophia.

I wasn't sure how to feel about Damon's gift, especially the fact that the simple platinum chain and a teardrop-shaped black diamond hanging from it was exactly something I would have picked for myself.

How could he read me so well and know I would have gravitated toward it in a store before something more extravagant or grandiose?

His knowing what I'd love only added to the guilt weighing on my shoulders about keeping him in the dark regarding my alibi for the night of Keith's murder.

It wasn't fair that to protect those weaker than me, I had to keep an integral part of who I was from someone who only wanted to protect me from the monsters of the world.

He was the one thing I'd always wanted my whole life. A person who'd put me first, wanted to keep me safe and believed me, even if things didn't make sense.

This whole situation sucked big hairy balls.

I tucked my arm into Damon's while guiding him toward the back of the room.

In the corner, a gorgeous woman with golden skin and a long mass of copper curls swayed back and forth as she hummed various tunes while the band around her prepped their instruments.

As I passed her, she smiled and tapped her elbow to mine. "Good to see you out."

"Thanks."

"Thought I'd let you know, the new track comes out next week."

"It was only a matter of time." I smiled at her, and then Damon and I continued to the stairs leading toward the VIP lounge.

"I take it you know each other?"

"You could say that. I invested in her indie

album project. She has one of the most soulful voices I've ever heard."

"Why not use your connections to get her in with a big label."

"She wants to stay indie. A big label would commercialize her and change her to appeal to the mass market."

"So she would rather play clubs instead of large venues?"

"If it makes her happier, why not?"

A group of models passed me, all of them no way in the vicinity of sober. Most were high on some substance or the other, by choice or through a cocktail they left unattended.

I shook my head and took the steps, letting Damon follow me.

It wasn't even ten o'clock. By the time it hit midnight, one of that crew, if not more, would be sitting in a corner passed out or rocking because they were jonesing for another fix.

The club was crawling with predators. I never let anyone buy me a drink or set my glass down at one of these shindigs.

I couldn't trust anyone, even my friends here. Sticking to sparkling water in the guise of a vodka tonic was better.

Man, I went through a lot of effort to hang

out with people I couldn't stand.

As we climbed the steps, tension seemed to radiate out from Damon.

"What's wrong?"

"Why do you do this?"

I glanced at him. "Do what?"

"Come to these events."

My eyes widened. Well, shit. I wished Damon would stop reading me like that.

"What makes you—"

"It's all over your face," he said, cutting me off. "I've watched you from the moment we arrived. You hate every second of being in this environment. Is all the time you spend with these people worth the energy it takes out of you?"

"This is part of my lifestyle. I'm a public figure. My job is for people to see me out and about at events."

"No, your career is based around clothing. You model it and design it. Those are the only times you have to be around this crowd. Being here is just an excuse to push buttons."

I abruptly stopped my climb to the second floor and whirled around to face him. Immediately, he grabbed hold of my waist before he collided with me.

With me a step above him, we were at eye

level. "Are we here for your analysis of my mental health, Dr. Pierce, or to figure out who could have framed me?"

"We can do both, Ms. Morelli. Avoiding the truth doesn't change it."

Irritation pushed at every nerve in my body, and the desire to stomp my stiletto into his toes sat high on my priority list.

"You want to talk about avoiding the truth? What about you? Tell me this need to protect me and watch over me isn't driven by your fixation on what happened to Maria? You couldn't save her from her choices, so you're determined to save me."

His jaw clenched. "You are not Maria. Your situation has nothing to do with her."

"Oh, really. 'Cause from where I'm standing, you still haven't let go of your guilt, and I'm dealing with the consequences. I refuse to go from one prison cell to another."

"What does that mean?"

"I don't care about the terms of my release. I don't need you with me twenty-four seven. We both have jobs. I navigated this life before you, and I'll manage after you."

Before I realized what he was doing, he fisted my hair and pushed me against one side of the stairwell wall.

"Let's get this straight. There is no after me. This is a done deal."

A chill slid down my spine.

I'd never let him turn me into someone like my mother. I'd never allow myself to become a woman trapped.

"I decide my future, Damon Pierce."

"I got you out of that jail cell. That means you're stuck with me now."

"You keep believing that. I would have found a way out. I don't need you to rescue me."

"What is it you need from me?"

"I need you to l—" I cut off my words as I noticed the people behind Damon.

"Sophia, I'm so happy to see you."

Damon stiffened at the sound of designer Karina Mehta's greeting. His attention still lay heavily on my face. However, my focus shifted to Karina.

Karina wore an off-the-shoulder dark green jumpsuit with a hint of shimmer. It fit her petite frame as if it kissed all her curves without being too tight, and she'd paired her outfit with a pair of sky-high needlepoint stilettos. The clothes were part of her newest collection.

She completed her look by pulling her jet-black hair into a slicked-back, high-top ponytail, which showed off her long, angular neckline and the chain of emeralds dangling from her ears.

Pushing Damon's arm down, I wrapped Karina in a hug. "It's nice to see a friendly face."

"Ignore all the cattiness. Next week, the gossips will have something new to chatter about." She turned to Damon, offering him her hand. "I believe we met briefly at my fashion show, Mr. Pierce. Has she worn it for you yet?"

"Worn what?"

He brushed his lips over her knuckles and said, "Not yet. We never seem to get the opportunity."

"That's too bad. Sophia's the reason I've had orders for other pieces."

"As long as no one asks Sophia to model them, I say congratulations."

I looked between the two. "You bought the sapphire and diamond bikini from Fashion Week?"

His gaze locked with mine, and the intensity made my throat dry. "Only I get the pleasure to see you wearing something like that, My Sophia."

"Seriously, you're insane." I turned my back to him and tucked my arm into Karina's.

Behind me, he said, "I thought you were the

insane one, and I carried the title of the psychopath."

I ignored him and ascended the stairs with Karina and her entourage.

When we reached the landing of the VIP area, Karina pulled me toward an alcove. "Let's go over here. I don't want anyone to overhear our conversation."

I glanced over my shoulder to see if Damon decided to follow us. Thankfully, a couple who seemed to know him waylaid him into a conversation.

The glare he shot in my direction told me he wasn't happy I'd left him behind, but I couldn't have cared less.

Too many eyes were on me, waiting for something to happen. And the whole place buzzed with speculation about me and all the nefarious ways I offed Keith that they were waiting to get a glimpse of anything they could use to spread through all the gossip channels.

Once Karina and I reached a high-top table in a corner, I propped an elbow on the wood and said, "Go ahead, ask."

"I know you didn't do it, so don't insult me by thinking I'd ask such a stupid question." Her annoyance should have made me feel better about the situation. Still, for some reason, it left an uneasiness churning in my gut.

"What makes you think I didn't do it?"

"Keith was scared shitless of you. There is no way in hell he would let you within ten feet of him to stab him through the heart."

"Stabbed him? Is that what everyone thinks happened to him?" I couldn't hide the surprise from my question, even though I knew I should have.

Who would have put that kind of information out to the public? Especially when the cops said it was poison. Was it all a lie? But for what purpose? There was no way I could overpower someone Keith's size.

No. No. I couldn't let my mind jump into an endless loop of questions without answers.

Damon and Lucian said it was poison, and I believed them. They were the tell the brutal truth type of men, so lying to me wasn't something they'd ever consider.

"I'm sure there is more to it than just a knife to the heart. Probably drugs and alcohol as part of the mix. I could name at least fifteen other people with bigger vendettas against the jackass"—Karina paused and made the sign of the cross with a smirk—"May he rest in hell. Me being one of them."

I frowned. "What did he do to you?"

"He stole my designs and then passed them off as his while we were in school. The professor knew what he'd done but did nothing about it because Daddy Randolph gave gobs of money as an endowment. Instead, the program director told me to keep my mouth shut or risk losing my scholarship."

"We've been friends for years. How do I not know any of this?"

"Because what he did to you and the other models is on a whole different level of fucked up than me. I'm only telling you this now to let you know there are many more suspects in the pool who the cops need to look at."

"I doubt you'd destroy your life for something he did to you in design school."

"True. Keith hated me for the sheer fact my career took off without the backing of a rich family. Then there's the shit that went down with Keith and Joseph." She gestured with her chin toward a man to our side with long white-blond hair, surrounded by models trying desperately to garner his attention.

I remembered hearing about a falling out between the two men but never delved deeper into it.

"What happened?"

She rolled her eyes. "Just a rinse and repeat of my story but on a public level. Keith accused Joseph of copying his designs when in reality, Keith stole Joseph's sketchbooks and released the collection before Joseph's line went into production. It was a big mess. And as always, Daddy Randolph used his media savvy to damage Joseph's reputation in the court of public opinion."

"I need to stay more informed on the gossip."

"I think you're getting into enough trouble right now." She cocked her head to the side, taking me in. "In fact, for a woman who spent some time in jail, you look remarkably good."

How could I look good after spending the last twenty-four hours aching for an orgasm? Irritation surged through me, and I glanced behind Karina to see where the bane of my existence was.

Well, wasn't that a surprise, he decided to do something else besides stalk my every move.

"I look rested because I drank a lot of water and had a good night's sleep."

She snorted at my response and shook her head. "You are such a liar. I think it has to do with that possessive lover of yours. I told you sex does great things for the skin."

If she knew so damn much, she'd know the asshole left me hanging and irritable.

I huffed. "Focus, Karina. Get back on topic."

"Just answer one question, and I'll let it drop."

"What?"

"Does he know you're in love with him?"

A hand settled on my waist, and then Damon spoke, "He suspects, but she needs to confirm it."

CHAPTER TEN

Damon

SOPHIA STIFFENED THE second my hands came around her waist, and she grew even more rigid after I gave my response to the designer's question.

I wanted the words from her. I needed to hear the words.

She had to know I wouldn't go to these extremes to protect her if I hadn't felt the same way.

"It's impolite to eavesdrop." Sophia tilted her head to the side, shooting me a pointed glare. "We were having a private conversation."

"Nothing is ever completely private when it's in a public venue. Wouldn't you agree, Ms. Mehta?"

Karina Mehta had watched me approach from behind Sophia. She wanted me to hear bits of their conversation, especially her last question. From my research into her background, she viewed Sophia as a close friend and would go to bat for her. Based on the conversation I overheard, she was privy to information about Sophia that Sophia rarely shared with others.

"Very true. Discussion at events like this stir chatter at other functions. It's a game."

"I don't care for games."

"You're with Sophia now. Playing the game is essential to her world." She smirked and then winked at Sophia, who furrowed her brow.

"Sophia and I understand what's required of the other, especially the games."

"Good to know. Let me know how you enjoy the piece you purchased from me." Karina leaned toward Sophia, whispered something in her ear, and kissed her cheek. "I'll see you soon."

Karina inclined her head in my direction as a goodbye. Then she moved toward her entourage, who waited on the side for her.

"You have fascinating friends."

"I do. Karina believes I'm innocent."

"You are."

"I am," Sophia nodded, keeping her dark eyes focused on me.

Then I continued, "But I still have questions about that night. I need to know where you went."

"Why? I wasn't involved in Keith's murder.

All we have to do is prove the evidence against me is circumstantial."

"I want no doubt in anyone's mind of your innocence. This means we need an airtight alibi of your whereabouts for that night."

"It's not important."

"The hell it isn't."

"Didn't you learn anything during your perusal of the crowd?"

"I learned plenty, but the information I want needs to come directly from you."

"Let it go, Damon."

"No." A prickle of something burned at the back of my mind. "Were you with someone? Is that the secret? We weren't together then. You left me, and I'd made it abundantly clear we had no future."

But the thought of any man having even a millisecond of her time gave me the urge to destroy the motherfucker, tear him limb from limb.

Pushing down the rage, I allowed the rational side of my mind to come forward. Even if Sophia was seeing someone else, I'd get him to back her alibi, and once the cops cleared her charges, I'd take care of the fucker.

"You can't be serious." The disbelief in her

onyx gaze calmed the turmoil lingering inside me.

"If not another man, then who were you with that night? I need something to prove your location during the times leading up to Randolph's murder and the hours after. A closed circuit feed from somewhere, a convenience store, a coffee shop, or a restaurant would do."

"Are you saying you can accept seeing a video of me going into another man's building and possibly doing something we've done if it proves my innocence?"

I clenched my jaw. "All I want is to show the evidence against you is bullshit. I'll deal with it no matter how the information comes."

She had to know this tactic she was using couldn't hide the fact she wanted to evade answering the question. And that it worked pissed me off.

She stepped toward me as emotions whirred in her nearly black eyes. "You confuse me."

"Welcome to the club," I muttered.

"This jealousy, this possessiveness over me, makes no sense. Why did you keep pushing me away if you wanted me."

"The same reason I gave you that first night we met. I'm the worst thing that can happen to you."

"How? You've never explained that statement."

I stared at her not saying anything. She couldn't be serious.

"Well?"

"I don't let go, Sophia. Once I claimed you, there was no escape. You run, I will catch you. If you hide, I will find you. You joked that I was a psychopath. When it comes to you, you have no idea how accurate you are."

And on top of everything else, all I'd brought was chaos to her life. If it wasn't my obsession with her, my need to protect her, Randolph wouldn't have targeted her for all the tabloid scandals of the last few weeks. Then whoever murdered the jackass wouldn't have the ammunition needed to set Sophia up for his murder.

She set a hand on my chest and parted her lips as if to say something, but she held them back when I shifted my body in front of her and focused on a pair of familiar faces at the far end of the room.

What were Henrietta Stanford and Rico Newman doing here? They were textile and interior designers I'd worked with in the past. They specialized specifically in wallpaper and window treatments for large scale building and interior home design projects. The last place I ever expected to see them was at a fashion industry event.

Sophia turned in the same direction and asked, "What are you looking at?"

"Former business acquaintances."

"Why do I feel you aren't very fond of them?"

"Because I'm not. They're a couple who don't show loyalty or discretion."

"Let me guess, they spilled information about one of your projects."

"They had access to a confidential project and then revealed information about the development to one of their clients. A week later, a reporter published an article about it in a national publication."

"How did you retaliate?"

"I didn't."

"Bullshit. You're Lucian's best friend. I know you did something."

I smirked. "I haven't given them any more of my business or referred them for other jobs."

"In other words, you had them blacklisted."

"I haven't said anything good or bad about them to anyone but you. We haven't crossed paths in well over three years."

"Let me guess, you plan to go say hello."

"Why not? We are here to mingle and investigate. Might as well chat with a pair of loose-lipped individuals."

"Oh, you want me to tag along while you play sleuth?"

I took her hand in mine. "I want you near me the whole time."

We weaved our way through the crowd. Every so often, someone would call Sophia's name, and every time, she nodded her acknowledgment and kept pace with me. To the average person looking at her, she seemed friendly yet aloof as she passed. However, I noticed the tightening of her lips, making it very evident she'd prefer not to engage with those people in any capacity.

Then there were those we walked by who made snide or derogatory comments as if we couldn't hear them about Sophia being a jailbird or wanted criminal. It had taken all of my willpower not to grab the offenders and clock them in the face.

However, Sophia kept her head up, seemingly unfazed.

The way Sophia constantly handled this bullshit spoke to her stamina in this world of excess I'd never comprehend.

As we neared my quarry, I studied them.

Henrietta Stanford and Rico Newman wore high-fashion attire in line with those around them. Gone were the conservative suits they favored to broker business for their textile design company. They fit well in this environment, and from how they socialized, they were well acquainted with many people around them.

It looked like they'd branched out into the glamorous side of design after I stopped taking their calls. However, it made me wonder why they hadn't pursued other lucrative real estate development clients outside my circle. The industry was thriving, and there was a great demand for those with experience in textile design.

"Stay a little behind me, and let me gauge what they're doing. Then I'll introduce you." I released my hold on Sophia's fingers.

As if annoyed by my suggestion, she pursed her lips. "Damon, you don't need to babysit me at every moment of the day. I can happily entertain myself. I know most of the people here. I promise not to leave without you."

"I don't trust a single person here, so you need to stay as close to me as possible."

"This is ridiculous. If I was perfectly safe while talking to Karina, what could happen to me within a few feet of you?"

"Plenty."

"For the love of God. You are seriously unbelievable." She shot daggers at me with her dark eyes. "I'm not sure what's worse, having you shackled to me at all times or sitting in a jail cell."

I tugged her forward so the front of her body brushed against mine. "If you want me to shackle you to my side, I have the means to do it. I have a feeling you would enjoy it."

"I have my doubts. Especially since you said, there is no chance of an orgasm in my imminent future."

"Give me what I want, and I'll give you all you can handle. You'll beg me to stop."

Her pupils dilated, and her lips parted to take an unsteady breath.

"That's coercion."

"I prefer to call it an incentive to cooperate."

She lifted up onto tiptoes and skimmed her palm over my shoulders and then around my neck. "I don't care what you call it. My answer won't change."

"Then I guess you'll continue to suffer."

"So will you. If I'm not getting any, neither are you."

"Oh no, that's not how this works. I will

continue to fuck you when I want, and I will continue to be the only one to come."

"We'll see about that." She pushed out of my arms, clenched her fist as if readying to punch me, and flipped her hair so dramatically that only she could pull it off without looking over the top. "Go do your thing, Mr. Pierce. I don't want you hovering. Come summon me when I'm needed."

Before I could respond, she tapped the person next to her on the shoulder and immediately began an animated conversation with them.

I resisted the urge to draw her back into our conversation. I'd pushed her to her limit, and it was time to pull back, no matter how much her temper heated my blood and rocked my self-control.

It was like a charge to the system, urging me to bend her over my knees and spank her, right here and right now, to show every one of the assholes in here how much she loved it when I made her ass glow for me.

Or push her down to the floor and suck me off as I'd done at Violent Delights. She'd looked so damn beautiful with tears pouring through mascara smudged eyes as I'd fucked her mouth, choking her with my cock, hitting the back of her throat over and over again.

By the time I'd finished with her, she'd been desperate to fuck, ready to come. No one in that club could have doubted that she was irrevocably mine.

She glanced my way as if sensing my thoughts, and her cheeks tinged a slight glow.

She narrowed her gaze and mouthed, "Wrong club," and continued whatever discussion she was engaged in.

I remained there for a few more moments, taking her in. My cock pressed hard against my pants, ready to tear through the material.

The woman fascinated me and scared me. She held a power over me no one else could ever claim before her.

She enthralled and seduced without trying, not just me but those around her.

She seemed to draw people to her even with the specter of rumors and speculation. Passersby saw her and came to say hello. Many seemed more acquaintances than friends.

She addressed everyone by name and engaged them in small talk, skillfully dodging any mention of the recent occurrences in her life. None of them noticed how her smile never truly reached her eyes.

Sophia Morelli, the center of attention and

hating every minute of it.

A pang of guilt hit me for telling her to wait until I called her to meet the textile designers.

Had I just done to her something her parents forced her to do by making her stay in the shadows until they wanted her to appear?

Fuck. I had no idea how to navigate anything anymore.

Before her, I knew the rules. I kept my emotions in check. A submissive had her place in my life. Sure, scenes, sex, and intimacy were all part of it. As a Dom, I would give myself to them as much as possible, but nothing went past the club.

Even with Maria, who I'd taken on as a long-term submissive, no part of me could conjure the deep-seated affection she needed. And the primal desire to protect had never become a factor in our relationship.

With Sophia, the depth of what I felt, my desires, and my need for her went to a visceral level I never knew existed. It was instantaneous and raw.

It drove me to do things I'd never do for anyone else.

Releasing a deep breath, I turned away from Sophia and moved toward the two textile engineers.

I studied Rico and Henrietta on my approach, taking in everything about them. The image they projected was one of a united front. Henrietta's dress seamlessly coordinated with Rico's suit from color to texture. No one looking at them would have any doubt they came as a pair. The only thing that made them stand apart was the stark contrast of their hair color. Rico had white, blond hair, while Henrietta's was a striking red.

Rico's blue eyes brightened in recognition when I neared. "Damon, it's been a long time. What are you doing here? I didn't think this type of place was your scene."

"I'm always up for a change of pace." I shook his hand and then inclined my head toward Henrietta.

"Good to see that you haven't become a hermit." Rico shot a glance toward Henrietta. "Though we couldn't blame you considering what we read about the new penthouse you built."

"The one you read about is just a prototype for a different building. You should know I'm not the type to give away the secrets to my personal living space."

Henrietta's mouth tightened around the edges as my words hit their mark. I wanted her to know that I remembered what she'd done.

Then she smiled. "You're smart to show a different property and keep your privacy. You can never be too careful."

Oh, the irony.

"Exactly."

"Who are you here with?" Henrietta scanned the area around me.

"My girlfriend. She is chatting with a few friends. She will find me sooner or later."

"You're dating someone in the fashion industry? I thought you preferred quiet relationships over ones with high-profile women."

What would she know about my relationships with anyone? We had only ever worked professionally, and for her to know even a tiny clue about my personal life meant someone from Violent Delights told her.

I cocked my head to the side, perhaps she saw me come in with Sophia.

No, that couldn't be it. Henrietta wouldn't have acted surprised to see me.

And from how she continued to search over my shoulder, she was looking for Sophia.

"What makes you think I'm with someone high-profile? Not everyone in the fashion industry is in the limelight."

"Is she a designer then?"

"Among other things."

"Speaking of designers," Rico interjected. "What is your opinion on the Keith Randolph murder?"

Of course, they'd want my take on the situation. Especially if they knew I was with Sophia.

"I prefer to keep my thoughts on the dead sex offender to myself. It's rather gruesome evening out conversation."

"Sex offender?" Henrietta took the bait I threw out. "You believe those rumors about him?"

"Why wouldn't I? It's an open secret in the industry. He's a known predator with multiple complaints."

"I wasn't aware of this." Rico watched me and then added. "Then again, I usually don't focus on rumors associated with clients."

And there I had my answer to Henrietta's statement about my dating history. They heard the rumors about Maria and my preferences at Violent Delights.

"I'm sure discretion is something your clients appreciate."

At that moment, the scent of Sophia's perfume touched my senses right before I felt her presence behind me. Moving to the side, I made space for her.

I watched Rico and Henrietta scan Sophia from head to toe, taking in everything about her and sizing her up. From the periphery of my eyes, it was easy to see Sophia hold herself with an air of confidence that pretty much told them to go fuck themselves with their perusal.

I drew Sophia closer to me. "Sophia, let me introduce you to Rico Newman and Henrietta Stanford. Rico and Henrietta, this is Sophia Morelli, my girlfriend."

"So, you're the Sophia Morelli everyone is talking about." Henrietta smiled as if she discovered something interesting.

Sophia glanced in my direction before she responded. "Yep, that's me, the troublemaker extraordinaire."

"I'm surprised you are here tonight."

"Why wouldn't I attend an event where I'm considered a VIP?"

"Mainly because of all the allegations against you."

Sophia's lips tightened the barest of a fraction, only someone who knew her every reaction would have seen it. "Which one are we talking about? I'm a fixture in the press after all."

"I'm referring to your recent incarceration. Some say they don't feel comfortable with you around them. Perhaps unsafe."

Every one of my instincts to protect Sophia surged forward.

Before I could go with my gut, she set her hand on my arm, telling me to stay out of it.

Sophia cocked her head slightly and then replied with a coolness to Henrietta that had me seeing a whole new side of her. "Are you saying you feel uncomfortable with me around you? You can hardly speak for the entire club since I've spent the evening with many people approaching me."

"It was an observation."

"Henrietta, I've never met you before. I don't know you, and we do not run in the same circles. Reading something in the tabloids isn't facts. Unless you've done something to me or my family, there is no reason for you to worry about—What's the word?" Sophia tapped her lip. "Yes, your safety."

"I wouldn't think so. I've never met you or anyone in your family before."

"Then you have nothing to worry about. Am I correct?"

"I have another question for you."

Sophia lifted a well-defined brow. "I'm sure you do."

"Is it true that you once said during a party that the best way for a Morelli to off someone is poison since no one would believe any of you would use that method?"

I jerked my attention to Sophia's face, and everything inside me froze.

She wouldn't have said something so incredibly stupid in public. She was a Morelli for God's sake. Making jokes like those in public could only cause her grief in the long run. Lucian had to have taught her better than that.

Wait.

Henrietta said poison.

For a split second I considered the possibility of Sophia killing Randolph and then trashed that thought. I just couldn't fathom her doing anything like that.

Besides, Randolph was paranoid when it came to Sophia. He wouldn't have let her close enough to get anything in him.

Still, she was hiding something. Could she know who killed Randolph and was protecting them?

Was that the reason she refused to tell me the truth? Or maybe she had killed him, and I was just fooling myself believing in her. After all, she was one of the most resourceful people I knew.

At that moment, Sophia's eyes lifted to mine. A rage like nothing I'd ever seen filled them, and she directed all of it at me.

Tears appeared for the briefest of moments, and then she schooled them away. Now, mixed with the anger facing me was hurt and pain.

Fuck, fuck, fuck.

I messed up more than I ever could possible with her.

I'd doubted her, just like everyone else in her life had. But what else could I do with all the secrets she kept from me?

She turned her attention away from me, focusing back on Henrietta and Rico. I reached for her, wanting to hold her back, just in case she decided to punch someone. I couldn't tell what she would do in this mood.

However, the glare she shot me told me to stay still.

"You need to get your facts straight before spreading rumors and lies loud enough for everyone around us to hear." She cocked a hand on her hip. "I never uttered a word of that statement. I wasn't even at the party where this statement came into being."

"Then who put it out there?" Rico challenged.

"Farah Lance. You know, the supermodel? We

are known for our escapades together. I'm sure you've seen the tabloids."

Henrietta laughed and then asked as if Sophia had just lied, "Why would she do that to you?"

"Because I refused to attend a party where the recently departed jackass was on the guest list. It was well known in the industry he enjoyed making me feel uncomfortable whenever he saw me."

She scanned the room.

"If you don't believe me, ask half the people in this room. Also, the same people around you are the ones to tell me all about the scene Farah made for standing her up. I believe she said something along the lines of me ditching her to take care of Morelli business and that my preferred method was the use of poison." Sophia tucked her hair behind her ear and stepped back. "Henrietta, Rico. I can't say it was good to meet you. You've made a terrible first impression. I hope we never see each other again."

Sophia turned and shot me a pointed glare. "I am going to find my way home. Don't follow me. I don't need or want you."

"Sophia, I'm—" She shoved my hand away and pushed past me, leaving me behind.

CHAPTER ELEVEN

Sophia

Pain seared through my chest as I descended the step to the bottom level of the club.

It took every ounce of my will to keep my face and posture void of emotion. The small break in my composure I gave to that bitch was as much of an insight into my life as I would let any gossip-mongers in the fashion industry get.

I refused to let anyone see how tired I was from constantly having to defend myself.

No matter what I did, the results were the same—I was alone.

Bile bubbled up into my throat as I recalled how Damon's body had gone rigid when that bitch asked about the poison.

Instead of questioning Henrietta's motives, he'd taken her words and considered the plausibility of whether or not I committed Keith's murder.

Maybe I was expecting too much from him.

Yes, I was keeping secrets, but love meant accepting the other without knowing all of the truth.

He was supposed to be the one person who believed in me when no one else would.

If I was his, wasn't that part of the deal?

I paused when I took the last step, looking toward the front door. So many papz camped in front of the club, waiting to take pictures of everyone going in and out. I had no energy for any of them.

The alley behind the building would take me directly to the design school. Only the tenants had access to that area.

Now, I had to find a way to get to it.

Slipping around a collection of servers preparing cocktails, I followed a busser into the kitchen.

Keeping my head up and faking that air of confidence I'd mastered over the years, I smiled at the staff, who stopped as they recognized me.

I strode past them and then blew a kiss at a line cook in the back of the area. A grin broke out on his face, and he blushed beet red. Then, the others around him started laughing and making comments to him.

With them all distracted, I pushed through a set of double doors and found the back exit leading to the alleyway.

When I hit the night air, I took a deep breath, lifted my face to the night sky, and let the first tear spill from my eyes.

I'd survive. I always had, and I always would.

Pushing down the heartache for the moment, I trekked through a maze of dumpsters, storage sheds, and parked cars until I reached the maintenance access for the school.

God, I hoped there was someone around to let me in. The last thing I wanted to do was use the front entrance of the school.

Just as I set my hand on the metal door, it popped open.

An older man with gray hair and kind brown eyes appeared. "Young Morelli, I knew I recognized you on the monitor. You're lucky I was down here to let you in."

"Thanks, Mr. Nelson. You're the best," I said to the evening head custodian.

"Don't get into too much trouble."

"You know me. I'm a good girl."

He chuckled. "Of course you are. Go on."

Less than a few minutes later, I entered the fabric room, hidden on the third floor.

Slipping my heels off, I set them against a wall with my clutch. I made my way through row after row of rolled fabrics in every color and pattern imaginable, towering to the ceiling. The scent of dyes and various design materials permeated through the air.

The school had five warehouses set up throughout the campus, but this one was my favorite. At the beginning of my modeling career and friendship with Karina, I'd spent countless hours here as her living mannequin, helping her with her projects and classes.

My time here with Karina helped me learn many skills I'd acquired to design clothes. It was like attending design school without a single day in the classroom.

On the other hand, the lessons I learned on the other side of the fashion aisle taught me just as many things, both good and bad.

If only the bad weren't so very bad and painful.

Walking over to a drafting table, I found the beginning sketches of a wedding gown. My thoughts immediately jumped to Eva and the wedding that all my drama currently overshadowed.

Deep down, I knew she wouldn't hold anything against me.

In my head, I could hear her tell me in her

silky, soft mother tone, "Sophia, don't be silly. I'd rather elope. All that matters is that I'm married before the baby arrives."

It still hurt my heart knowing my issues had put a cloud over the joy she should feel.

I clenched my eyes tight and dropped my head.

It was so much easier to focus on other people and how my fuckups hurt them than face the pain I felt, knowing I would forever remain alone.

Maybe Mom had it right. She pretended to feel nothing and focused on everything but her emotions. More than likely, that was how she survived with her sanity, being married to Dad for decades.

What was the world coming to if I felt sympathy for my mother?

Shaking the insanity from my mind, I muttered, "Time to end this fucking night and go home."

I took one last look at the sketch and turned but abruptly stopped when I found Damon only a few feet from me.

"You aren't going anywhere unless I'm with you."

✧ ✧ ✧

My heartbeat thundered in my chest as I stared at Damon. His green eyes blazed as if I were the one to have done him wrong.

Inhaling a steadying breath, I allowed the hurt coursing through my body to morph into rage. It was better than the tears I so desperately wanted to spill seeing Damon and knowing he wasn't the man I believed he was.

He wouldn't get those.

I refused to let him see my pain.

"How did you find me?"

"Your phone. I can track it."

"Well, you can stop tracking it. You are no longer part of any equation involving me. Your services are no longer needed, Mr. Pierce."

"Services?" He lifted a brow, humor lighting his eyes and sending a flutter through my belly. "That's an interesting way to put what I do for you."

"You don't do anything for me. Not anymore."

"That's not a decision you get to make. Remember, I put a lot of money on the line for you."

"I have a hefty trust fund. I am more than capable of cutting you a check. Then we can go our separate ways."

"Tsk. Tsk." He shook his head. "It doesn't work that way between us. You chose me. That means I'm not going anywhere."

The intensity with which he stared at me made me feel stalked. Hunted.

"You don't trust me. You don't believe in my innocence. Why would you want to be with me?"

"Because I do."

I cocked a hand on my hip. "Not a good enough answer. Have a good life, Damon."

"Oh, you want a better reason. I'll give you a much better reason." He prowled toward me like a feral tiger slowly approaching his prey. "I claimed you. You belong to me, and I'm not letting you go."

His words ignited a painful throbbing between my legs.

Instead of focusing on how my traitorous body reacted to his presence, I stated, "I choose not to belong to you."

"Is that right?"

"Did I stutter?"

"Sophia, Sophia, Sophia. It's too bad you didn't read the fine print." He moved within touching distance, and it took all my strength not to retreat.

"Why don't you fill me in."

"Once you sign on the dotted line, there is no backing out of the deal." As he drew closer, a smirk touched the corners of his full mouth. "Are you scared of what I'll do to you when I get my hands on you, Sophia?"

A pulse of arousal shot through me, making me want to smack myself for wanting him when he'd devastated my heart.

"I'm not scared of anyone, and you aren't getting your hands on me ever again. Accept it, Damon, it's over." I lifted my chin, knowing full and well how this would end.

"We aren't even close to over." He grabbed hold of my wrist and jerked me toward him, and I countered, tugging my arm free as some sense pushed through the sexual haze.

I gasped in the air and narrowed my eyes. "You don't get it. You don't make the decisions for my life, Damon Pierce. I get to choose what I want."

"You chose me."

"Well, I'm changing my mind since it looks like I suck at making decisions when it comes to men."

I pressed my fingertips to my eyes, not wanting to look at him when I said, "I saw your face when that woman made her statement about the poison. Her words made you question my innocence."

Remembering the pain I'd felt, what I still felt washed away a good portion of the desire thrumming in my system.

"I shouldn't have let anything put doubts in my mind."

"That's exactly the point. I won't be with someone who doesn't trust me, who doesn't give me the benefit of the doubt, who thinks I'm a liar."

"I don't think you're a liar. I'm sorry, Sophia. I fucked up."

"You fucked up. Is that what you call it? Yeah, you fucked up." Raw, volatile anger surged forward. "But you know what?"

He said nothing, only watched me with those vivid green eyes.

My lips trembled, and tears poured down my cheeks when I said, "I fucked up even more because I knew better and still opened my heart to you. I allowed myself to fall in love with you. I should have known sooner or later you'd let me down like everyone else has most of my life."

The second the words left my lips; I regretted saying them. How could I be so stupid to let him see any more of my hurt and pain? Why was I making myself more vulnerable to him?

Exhaustion settled onto my shoulders.

I no longer had the stamina to defend myself and fight for people to see or accept the real me.

All I wanted was to go home, put on a pair of pajamas, and hide under the covers in my bed.

But where was home? My apartment wasn't safe, especially with the media constantly trying to sneak into my building, and the thought of going back to Damon's wasn't something I could handle.

I could always call Lucian or Eva.

They'd take me in no matter how much I screwed up my life.

"I was irritated with you for keeping secrets and allowed it to cloud my judgment. I promise you, I don't believe a word Henrietta or Rico said."

I wanted to say, *"That was because I gave you and the entire club a way to prove my truth,"* but I held those words in.

Instead, I said, "I'm not sure I'm strong enough to change what happens the next time someone questions my integrity with something I could have plausibly done."

I turned my back to him. I couldn't face him anymore. Through blurry vision, I peered up at the rows and rows of fabrics in every shade of red.

Even this room had lost its haven status in my soul. Now, it would only remind me of my heartache.

Inhaling deep, I straightened my shoulders. "I need to break this hold you have on me while I still have the ability to move on. Let me go."

"I can't. You have the same hold over me. Why can't you see it?"

"What are you talking about? You never show it." I said, turning to face him.

"You are the only woman I have gone to such great lengths to protect. Until you, I didn't know the type of emotions coursing through my body even existed. Your safety and your happiness are a priority for me. If you only knew the number of times, I've faced off against your brother for you. You will always come first."

A tremor shook my body, and my lips quivered as more tears poured from the corners of my eyes.

"Are you saying what I think you're saying?"

"Tell me what you're hearing."

"My hold on you is that you're in love with me."

His green irises burned into mine as if I stared directly into a raging fire. After a few seconds, he swallowed and then nodded.

"Damon," I whispered.

"Sophia."

I wasn't sure who moved first. All I knew was that our hands were on the other within seconds, and his mouth covered mine.

This kiss wasn't anywhere near soft or sweet. It scaled closer to all-consuming and branding. Our tongues dueled, tasting, savoring, consuming. Damon nipped and bit my lower lip, leaving a delicious sting meant to coax my desire higher.

He fisted my hair and walked me backward until he pinned me to the rack of red fabrics. He scored his teeth down the column of my throat and neck, making goose bumps prickle all over my skin.

I wanted to touch him, trace his muscles, get him naked. But he held my arms immobile, taking all of my control.

Breaking our embrace, he stared at me, face flush, breath coming out in short pants, eyes dilated, turning them into rings of bright green. The untamed, feral desire on his face had my breast swelling and nipples beading into painful peaks.

As he kept his heated gaze on me, he tugged the front zipper of my dress down, exposing my black lace bra and matching thong. Then, he pushed the straps of my dress down my shoulders, letting the designer material pool at my feet before tracing his fingers over my collarbone, between my cleavage, and up to my throat.

The press of his fingers along the column of my neck sent my mind and body into a riot of painful desire and need.

His man possessed the ability to seduce with his mere presence or the slighted touch. When his focus was on me, I saw nothing but him.

He skimmed his lips over mine and murmured, "You are so fucking beautiful."

"Damon," was all I could say.

He cast a spell over me, locking me inside. I had no desire to escape.

A shiver slid down my spine when he reached above my head, where a loose length of crimson silk hung from different rafters.

The racks behind me held thousands of pounds of expensive fabrics, making them secure and something he could use to keep me in place.

I scanned the perimeter of the room. There had to be cameras in here, keeping surveillance. There was even a possibility of a security guard sweeping the area on a routine inspection.

A pang of unease tickled my stomach. Could I

risk more tabloid scandals? It was already too late. I stood before this man, nearly naked, while he was fully clothed.

Then, my attention returned to Damon, and all my worries disappeared. Nothing else mattered but us.

This was my lover and me. Raw, without filters, pure.

"Tell me no if this isn't what you want, Sophia."

I licked my lips and responded, "I'm not letting you out of this. You owe me multiple orgasms."

"Is that right?" A wicked smile touched his lips.

"You got yours. I want mine. I will find a way to pay you back if you don't make restitution."

"You do hold a grudge, don't you?"

"When it's warranted."

"How many do you want?" He wound the first bits of silk around one arm, securing it to the rafter, then he pulled more fabric free from another bolt and repeated the process with the other.

The urge to say as many as I could get sat on the tip of my tongue, but then I remembered his treat of making me beg him to stop. And knowing

Damon, he'd make it his mission to torture me with relentless orgasms, even if it meant continuing his non-stop ministration on my body until the students came in for classes in the morning.

"I'm waiting for an answer. I'm positive you know that your threats of payback do not affect me."

"You are too damn cocky for your own good, Damon Pierce."

"I am who I am. Now be a good girl and answer the question."

"Three."

He lifted a brow as if surprised by my number. "I'll take that as a minimum."

"You have to be kidding me. I'll die by the end of the night."

"Death by orgasm. I'm sure Lucian will spare my life knowing you bore a smile on your face during your ultimate demise."

"Don't bring my brother into this. That's just gross."

"We met at his kink club, Sophia. He's well aware that I fuck the hell out of you."

"Let's pretend he doesn't." I scrunched my nose up, which had him shaking his head. "I prefer to keep sex and any of my siblings in two very distinct categories."

He rubbed his thumb over the crease that formed between my brows and then leaned down and kissed my forehead. "Anything for you, My Sophia."

He looked around him and then shot me a wicked smile, moving to a small section with what looked like red rope. He inspected several spools before making his selection and returning to me.

"What are you planning to do with that?"

"I remember your interest in Shibari. Especially how your cheeks flushed and you pressed your thighs together as scenes progressed with those couples."

A spasm rocketed through me, and a shiver slid down my spine.

It was the night Damon claimed me at Violent Delights, making it so no other Dom would ever touch me or look my way.

The evening had started with me wanting to escape all thoughts of Damon Pierce. He'd rejected me, so I decided to explore with someone else. But there was no replacing him, and I ended up watching a Japanese rope bondage demonstration. The couples were beautiful and oh-so sensual. I'd lost myself in the art and intimacy of it.

"Are you going to recreate the patterns on

me?"

"I'm not a rope master by any means, but neither am I an amateur." The throbbing in my core intensified, hearing the lust in his voice, "Want to see how aroused you get when you're the rope model?"

There was no thinking twice about my answer. "Yes."

"Then we begin. Make sure to breathe naturally." He kissed my forehead and picked up a bundle of rope he had set on a shelf near him.

First, he encircled my waist and then made tiny knots from my belly button upward, stopping right between my breasts.

He pulled the rope across my breast and around again before creating a pattern around my bra-covered breast that squeezed and constricted. My nipples puckered, and a pinching sensation filled my body.

Goose bumps prickled my skin, and a flood of desire pooled between my legs.

I couldn't help but shift, making the bindings tighter.

"Easy," Damon crooned and slid his fingers between the rope and my body as if to ensure it wasn't damaging my skin. "Want to keep going?"

Nodding, I stared into his deep green eyes and

lost myself in the experience he constructed for me.

He set his hands on my hips and pushed my underwear down. Immediately, my pulse skyrocketed to an unsteady tempo. Reaching over to his side, he grabbed another bundle and continued his sensual tantalization.

By the time he finished, he had me completely at his mercy. Red silk tethered my arms to the rafters above my head, crimson ropes weaved, intricate geometric designs all over my chest and torso, and every thought in my body centered on the ropes he had positioned on either side of my labia. Every sway, shift, breath, heightened the sensations on my clit.

The evil man even bound my legs in a way that kept them apart and restricted any attempt to close them.

I was desperate to come, and there seemed no relief in sight. The slightest glide of Damon's fingers or caress of his body would surely send me over. Hell, maybe even a breeze could do it.

"Soon, Sophia," he promised, stepping back to study me.

That was when I noticed the feral, unguarded lust on his face and the heavy presence of his erection pressing against the inside of his pants.

"You have a gorgeous cunt. I love how it weeps down the inside of your thighs, soaking through the threads of the hemp."

"Stop staring at me and do something."

He strolled toward me. "How do you want your pleasure? Immediate and relieving or with a bite of pain and longer lasting?"

My core contracted, and my bound nipples tightened against the hemp around them.

My mind clouded as my need catapulted higher.

"Is there really a choice?"

He narrowed his eyes and then grabbed my thighs, hooking my knees over his shoulders. "No, there isn't."

His mouth depended on my exposed pussy, and I threw back my head as the insanity of sensation engulfed me. His tongue dived deep into my channel, thrusting in and out.

He used his thumbs to put pressure on the ropes positioned on the outside of my pussy lips to squeeze the aching nub at the apex of my sex.

Everything heated inside me. I couldn't think. Damon ate at me in a rhythm meant to keep me right on the cusp.

Bastard.

I was there, almost there. He knew it. He

fucking knew it.

Then his mouth shifted, his teeth bit my exposed clit while, at the same time, he plunged three fingers into me.

A guttural cry escaped from my mouth as my pussy contracted, spasming and flexing. The pain, the ache, the euphoric pleasure cascaded through me, on the cusp of overwhelming. I gasped for air, unable to breathe. I thrashed against my bonds, and sweat dripped down my belly as goose bumps prickled my skin.

It was too much and just not enough at the same time.

His fingers wouldn't cut it. I needed more of him.

"I need your cock. Damon, give me your cock. Please," I begged, not caring that I whined and moaned out of desperation.

"Not yet. I want more."

"You can have more later."

"No. You had demands. I live to serve." His lips closed over my clit, making me buck and writhe.

He fucked me with his mouth and fingers until I came twice more, gasping and begging him to give me what I wanted.

Pulling his hand free of my pussy, he stood

and unzipped his pants, freeing his beautiful hard length.

A bead of precum glistened from the tip, and my mouth filled with saliva for a taste.

"I changed my mind. I want to suck you off."

"You said you wanted this. You're getting every bit of my cum tonight."

He hooked an arm around one of my thighs and took his thick, hard length into his hand, stroking himself from root to tip.

The sight of him had my throat going dry. He oozed power and virility in a way I'd never seen on anyone else.

He moved in closer, brushing along the ropes, making them squeeze my clit. It was a maddening and oh-so-wonderful sensation.

Slowly, he nudged my still quivering opening as if testing my readiness. Then, instead of sinking balls deep as I expected, he teased me, rocking back and forth with shallow penetration. At the same time, his thumb circled my swollen and sensitive folds in a wicked dance.

He never touched my aching clit, only came the barest point to graze it.

I whimpered and moaned, conveying my need, but it only made him chuckle.

Bursts of heat bloomed inside me, and the

walls of my sex tensed, desperate and ready for that one hard thrust that would send me over.

"You're mine, Sophia."

I writhed, lifting my hips in a futile attempt to draw him in. "I know."

"It's impossible for me to let you go. Even if the best thing for you is to do just that."

"I know."

"You don't have a fucking clue." He plunged deep into me.

"Oh God," I screamed as my back bowed, and I immediately my pussy clamped down on him, tumbling me into another mind-blowing release.

I clenched my eyes tightly closed as the incredible pleasure of his invasion engulfed my senses.

In this position, bound and spread open for him, I felt so full, so stretched, unable to take anything but what he gave me. It was blissful, etched with a tinge of pain from the ropes, from the constriction, from the tethering of my arms, and I loved every moment of it.

My core continued to pulse and tremble as he took hold of my other thigh and started his ruthless assault on my pussy.

He fucked me like a man possessed as if he wanted to mark me as his, brand me in some way.

The binding around my body tightened with each pounding thrust. The expensive material squeezed and chafed my skin, adding to the erotic insanity of what we were doing.

I had no doubt I'd bear marks from this experience. I wanted them. I needed them.

"Say the words. I need to hear them," Damon demanded through gritted teeth.

Sweat covered his brow, and a deep flush covered his face.

Fear and worry still fought me, but I knew there was no holding back anymore.

I lowered my mouth to his and whispered, "I'm in love with you, Damon Pierce."

CHAPTER TWELVE

Damon

"I LIKE THE way it looks on my skin."

I shifted my attention from where I massaged the reddened marks on Sophia's thighs to her flushed face.

The haze of lust had yet to leave her onyx irises, and her breath remained unsteady.

"This wasn't the right place to push things this far. Before we leave, I'll have one of my people grab the surveillance footage of this room."

She ran her hands along one of the bundles of rope I'd used on her body, caressing it. "I have no complaints. And from the way your cock remains rock hard. You're primed and ready to service me again."

"What happened to you saying my services were no longer necessary?"

"I think I've changed my mind. You do have your uses." She reached forward and cupped my erection, fisting me through my pants, up and down.

Staying her movement, I said, "I'm going to service you by making you choke on my cock if you don't stop that and shut up."

"Promise?"

I grabbed hold of her face, bringing mine right up against hers. "Stop playing with fire, or you'll get burned."

"I know you want to do it." She licked her lips, making me crave to bite them and watch them swell as tears pooled in her eyes.

"What is it you think I want to do?"

"You want to push me to my knees like you did in the club and fuck my face. You want anyone who watches us on that security camera that recorded us, that is continuing to record us, to know I belong to you."

If she only knew the true depths of her words. The primal desire to mark her as irrevocably mine hummed through my blood. I wanted every-fucking-body in the world to know.

I bound her to the rafters and fucked her mindless, giving me one and her multiple mind-blowing orgasms, and it still wasn't enough.

"How did you come to this conclusion?"

"First, you claimed me, remember? You'd put a sign on my forehead that says "belongs to

Damon Pierce" if I let you. Second, you're a control freak, and I challenge you at every turn and refuse to give you the things you have always gotten with everyone else."

"And those are?"

"Unfettered access into my life. I don't answer questions when you ask. I don't do what you tell me as soon as you say them. And you can't fit me into any of your little boxes."

"If you know that's what I want, why do you make it harder for me?"

Something passed over her features, and immediately, the lighthearted mood disappeared.

"Because my life isn't about making everything easier for you. I am going to make things easier for me. I know I can be a brat, but that is a game we play, and it turns you on. I know my worth."

"Are you saying the women before you didn't know their value?"

"Not at all. Your previous women bent for you too easily because you are you. You overwhelm and intoxicate. You do it to me. Today's situation was an example. I got too wrapped up in you and learned how badly you can hurt me." She pushed my hands away and moved to pick up her dress. "I won't forget again that I want you but don't need you. It's a hard lesson to learn."

Turning back to me, she stepped into her clothes, adjusted the straps, and pulled up the front zipper.

"I'm sorry, Sophia."

"I won't be a pawn in anyone else's life. I won't let you use my passion or love to manipulate me."

"I wouldn't do that. What have I done to make you think that?"

Over her shoulder, she said, "You want evidence to prove my innocence instead of accepting my word. Nothing you say will convince me otherwise."

"I told you that I believed you."

"Bullshit." She whirled around. "I won't ever forget the suspicion I saw on your face when she made those accusations."

"I fucked up."

"Oh well, now at least I know that no matter how you feel about me, it won't ever stop you from having doubts about me."

The cool, detached way she delivered her words revealed more about how I hurt her than I realized.

Brick by brick, I saw her reinforcing the walls she used to protect herself.

No fucking way, not from me.

"I don't doubt you. You know what you are to me."

"Do I?" She lifted a brow. "Then tell me, do you still want to know where I was the night the asshole died? Lie to me and tell me you don't. Go ahead. I'll wait."

I gritted my teeth.

She'd backed me into a corner.

I wouldn't lie to make things easier, and in this situation, even if I was, there was no salvaging things. She knew the truth. I wanted to know. I had to know.

It wasn't as if I had some nefarious motive behind everything.

Her protection and her safety came first.

"Dammit, Sophia. It has nothing to do with me not believing in you. I want to keep you from going to jail. Why can't you see that?"

"Oh, I see plenty. Until the incident in the club, I thought you were the only person who ever took anything I ever said at face value. There is no convincing me that any of what you're saying is true." She shrugged, strode to where her underwear lay on the ground, picked it up, and walked toward the door. "Honestly, I'm glad reality decided to slap me in the face. It's easier to accept how my life will go moving forward."

"Want to explain what any of that means?"

"You're the one who said I picked you, and now I have to deal with it. At least my rose-tinted glasses cleared up, and I continued this with wide-open eyes. It really sucks when I find myself feeling compassion for my mother and the choices she made when all she's done is view me as a disappointment."

Without giving me a backward glance, she strode to the doors and walked out.

✧ ✧ ✧

TWENTY MINUTES AFTER leaving the design school, Sophia and I crawled through traffic, making our way to my penthouse.

Neither of us had spoken a single word to the other since her dramatic exit from the fabric room. However, a heavy layer of tension blanked the energy between us.

Most of it probably came from my direction. She'd fucking written us off as another couple like her parents.

I'd seen it in her eyes. No, not just seen it. She said it by implying she understood Sarah Morelli's choices.

Fuck that shit.

Bryant and Sarah Morelli were two people who held no trust for the other, who found some obvious physical attraction together considering the number of children they produced, but they had nothing of substance.

My hands clutched the steering wheel, my irritation with the whole situation boiling my blood.

Sophia had accused me of trying to use her feelings to manipulate her. Was that how her fucked up father kept his wife under his thumb?

She couldn't possibly believe we were anywhere in the same vicinity of that toxic, hateful relationship.

The mere thought of it was like a slam to the gut.

All I asked for were the answers to the questions about her alibi.

She expected me to have complete faith in her, but she couldn't trust me with her secrets.

I had a right to know, especially after all the shit I'd jumped through to get her out of jail.

I gripped the back of my neck, needing to ease the tension in my muscles.

I glanced in her direction. Her attention remained straight through the front windshield, barely shifting an inch since we entered the car.

What the fuck was she hiding?

When I asked her if it was another man earlier in the night, she'd never straight out denied the possibility.

Who would she have found to replace me?

What the hell was wrong with me? There was no other man. She'd waited twenty-five years for her first sexual experience. She wouldn't jump from me to someone new so fast.

It was time to stop allowing my emotions to supersede rational thought.

Then again, maybe I needed to give myself a little bit of leeway. Until now, I'd never had Sophia Morelli in my life. She pushed buttons I didn't even know I had.

Logically, I damn well knew there was no one else. Still, the vision of eliminating every fucking jackass who chanced to look in her direction lived rent-free in my head.

The sooner we got home, the better. I needed to find a way to calm my agitation.

Hopefully, a few dozen laps in the rooftop pool would do the trick. If not, I'd fuck the hell out of Sophia. It was the least she deserved for keeping me in the dark about every-fucking-thing about that night Randolph died.

Sophia's phone buzzed.

With a resounding sigh, she opened her clutch, pulled out her cell, and read her message.

She stared out the window for a few moments before she responded, set the mobile back inside her purse, and relaxed on the headrest, closing her eyes.

Resignation and sadness washed over her features. Immediately, my instinct to protect her surged. No matter the depth of my irritation with her, she was mine to protect.

"Upsetting news?" I asked, breaking the silence.

She pinched the bridge of her nose. "Something like that. I can never catch a break."

"Meaning?"

"Meaning, a group chat with people wanting to know if I'm okay."

"Why is that a bad thing?"

"Because they are fellow models who like to spread gossip. They heard about the incident at the club." She turned her face in my direction. "And want to verify the information their source gave them."

"Can I assume you said no comment?"

She glared at me and then turned away to stare out of the side window. "Once in a while, I prefer not to be the center of attention, keep a low profile, and have people talk about something other than me for a change. But alas, it wasn't meant to be."

"Do I detect that bit of snark directed in my direction?"

"Of course not, Mr. Pierce. I was already the talk of the town. You know, with that murder thing hanging around my neck like a fifty-ton weight. I'm sure I would have run into that twat who caused that scene if I attended the fashion show alone as I intended."

"Didn't you once tell me that your life was high profile and media comes with the territory?"

"Yeah, well, sometimes the media darling needs to wallow in self-pity and wish she became a nun instead of a fashion model at eighteen."

"Self-pity is for the weak. You aren't weak."

"So wallowing is out, but joining the local order is still in?" She shrugged. "I'm sure my parents will rejoice."

"The last thing I wish you to become is a nun, especially since I'm your Dom and enjoy fucking the hell out of you every chance I get."

My cock jumped as that charge of energy pulsed to life whenever either of us felt that draw of desire.

The way Sophia fidgeted in her seat said she

felt it, too.

"If I decided to join a convent tomorrow, would my nun status keep you from touching me?"

"Sophia, if you were a nun the first time I met you, it still wouldn't have stopped me from touching you. Our attraction is too visceral to ignore." I set a hand on her thigh and slid it up to her bare pussy, stroking her slick seam.

Fuck. I loved how aroused she became with the slightest provocation.

"You truly have no fear of God's wrath, do you?"

"Nope. And since I've already got a reservation scheduled for eternal damnation, I'd make sure to thoroughly defile you in said convent before I kidnapped you from under the Mother Superior's nose."

As if on instinct, she parted her legs to give me better access, and I pressed my fingers deeper, finding her clit and circling it.

Her hands grabbed hold of the armrests, and nails dug into the leather. Through the thin fabric, her hard nipples pushed at the material, making my mouth water to bite and tease.

"I know what you're doing," she accused.

"What am I doing besides teasing your cunt,

still slick from my cum?"

"You're trying to distract me from the texts." She responded with a huskiness that revealed her very aroused state and lifted her hips, trying to force my fingers to a spot she desired. "You do know a lot of women are offended by the word cunt."

"Good thing you aren't one of them." I pulled into a parking space near my private elevator, moved my seat back, and then adjusted to watch her as she writhed with her knees spread wide and pussy exposed.

"You're very cocky."

"It's not cocky when my big dick is a fact, and so is the certainty that I'm shoving it down your throat in a minute and planning to make you choke on it."

Her eyes widened and then narrowed. "You think so?"

"I know so. Now shift the car into park if you don't want me to move my hand."

Without telling her twice, she followed directions, her breath growing more unsteady by the second.

Once she set the automobile into a safer situation than what I had planned for her, she asked, "W-what now?"

"You know exactly what."

Her pupils dilated, swallowing her irises and turning them almost entirely black as onyx before she asked, "Here?"

I stared at her, giving her no response.

Maybe it was the lingering agitation with her about the secrets she refused to tell me, but I wanted to push her.

I'd fucked her face in front of the club members, but here in the parking garage, just like at the fashion school, edged on that discovery of society at large, making it irrevocably known that she belonged to me.

But then again, anyone seeing her as I saw her was unacceptable. That was why every recording of us would stay in our private collection for our viewing only.

By morning, I'd have any trace of our escapade in the fabric room erased from all security servers.

"I know what you're doing?" She unfastened her seat belt, taking my hand from between her legs and setting it on my lap.

Then she tucked her legs underneath her and reached over to open my pants. First, she slowly unbuckled my belt and opened the button of my pants. Then she lowered the zipper before tugging at the expensive cotton of my underwear.

"What am I doing?"

"You want the cameras to record our upcoming activities?" She gestured with her chin to the one pointed directly down through the windshield of the sports car. "Tell me I'm wrong? It turns you on."

"You're not wrong. And the idea of others watching us excites you, too." Her fingers closed around my cock, and I couldn't help but throw my head back at the incredible feel of her stroking me as she pulled me out. "Now, you'll tell me if I'm wrong."

"I admit nothing." Using her index finger, she rubbed the precum dripping from the slit at the tip of my cock in circles around the crown.

"Of course you don't. You hold back while I have to lay myself raw for you."

Something passed in her dark gaze, and she said, "Fine, I confess. The idea of watching me suck you off turns me on."

"Then I suppose you will enjoy seeing a copy of the surveillance footage of our earlier activities from the fashion school, too. I have to say, getting an eagle-eye view of me fucking you while you're bound and at my mercy has its appeal."

She held my stare as her breath coasted over

the bulbous head of my dick, followed by a flick of her wicked tongue. "As long as it's for a private showing with you and me as the only audience members, I have no objections."

Fisting her hair, probably harder than necessary, I ordered, "Open."

An impish smile touched her lips as her lips parted, and she engulfed me, taking me all the way back.

However, instead of waiting for further instructions, she swallowed, contracting the back of her throat, causing me to hiss, "Fuck," and dig my fingers into her scalp.

A moan escaped her lips, vibrating around me, and she squirmed in her seat.

Knowing I was the only man to experience her mouth brought out a possessiveness unlike anything I could describe.

She leveraged one arm on the middle console to help her balance, and the other pumped my cock.

Warm wet heat worked me up and down, laving the sensitive crown of my dick. Her tongue ran the length of the thick vein along the base of my cock with each pass.

The intensity of pleasure began to envelop every one of my senses, and the drive to fuck began to surge.

I guided her in the rhythm I wanted, needed, and craved. It pushed me closer and closer to the point of no control.

I made the mistake of looking down at her face. Tears streamed along her cheeks, and mascara smudges stained the skin under her eyes. Her red-painted lips glistened with saliva as they flared around me.

Immediately, my tempo changed, and I pumped up into her as I tugged her head forward.

A guttural whimper came from her as I held her immobile for a few seconds with each pass. It was brutal and fucked up, and I loved every second of it.

And from seeing her hand between her legs, working to soothe herself, she got off on my cruelty.

"You have no idea how much I love seeing those tears."

Feeling my balls draw up, I pulled her off my cock. Confusion immediately filled her dark, desire-clouded eyes.

Then I lifted her, pulling her legs astride me, and thrust in.

"Damon," she cried out and grasped my shoulders as her back bowed.

Her gorgeous tits bounced in the confines of her dress right at my eye level, a beautiful tease to the senses.

I fucked up into her, not giving her the chance to set the pace. I pulled her down into each lift of my hips like a man possessed.

"Oh God, Damon. You're so deep. I'm there. More. Please."

"What do you want? I can't give it to you, if you don't tell me."

"I don't know." She shook her head from side to side. "I don't know. Please."

She held onto me, bucking and begging. I slid the fingers of one hand down the cheeks of her ass, aiming for her puckered hole, while the thumb of the other strummed her clit.

The instant I pushed into her, she erupted around my cock, crying out her release. Her cunt clamping down on my pistoning cock so hard, it made it almost impossible to move.

The flex and contractions of her pussy muscles seemed to roll in an undoing spiral and when her nails scored down the back of my neck, guaranteeing marks, if not a bit of blood loss, what little rein I had left on my cock disappeared. I rutted up into her, letting loose and coming in hard, hot shots of cum deep into her quivering cunt.

CHAPTER THIRTEEN

Sophia

"Wow. You look like a supermodel version of a fertility goddess," I said to my older sister, Eva the moment she crossed the threshold of Damon's penthouse.

She wore a form-fitting midnight blue maternity dress that hit just above the knees and showed off her beautiful and huge baby bump. The calf-length, high-heeled leather boots she paired with the outfit gave her a sophisticated vibe.

Then again, Eva was the epitome of elegance and sophistication.

"You are wonderful for my ego." Eva kissed my cheek and then rubbed her stomach. "This kid of mine thinks there is unlimited space in there."

"You are all belly. In other areas, no one would even know you are pregnant. I have your gown in the spare bedroom so we can make the last adjustments and leave some room just in case you get bigger."

She sighed. "I will fall over if I get any bigger."

"If you keep wearing three-inch heels you will."

She pursed her lips, giving me the side eye. "I can guarantee that when you have children, you'll strut around town in the latest fashions and heels until you deliver your kid."

Just her mentioning the possibility of me having a baby made my stomach twist in knots.

My life was in so much turmoil, I could barely keep my head above water with all the messes I found myself wading through. And on top of everything, I wasn't sure there was a future for Damon and me.

Pushing my thoughts aside, I focused on Eva and realized she caught my reaction to her statement.

Damn, Eva and her mother hen, eagle eyes. "Let's table the pregnancy talk. All of the stress for the last few weeks can't be easy on you. I want to know how you are doing?"

"As well as can be expected, living locked up in this ivory tower of mine." I gestured to the area around me.

"What do you mean locked up?" The worry in

Eva's question had me tucking an arm in hers and guiding her toward the living room area.

"Don't panic. I'm fine. According to the terms of my bail, Damon is responsible for me at all times, so he feels he has to be with me everywhere I go. It just gets annoying sometimes."

A crease formed between her brows, but she kept whatever passed in her thoughts to herself and asked, "Where's Damon right now?"

"At the gym. It connects to the penthouse so we can do our thing with the fitting while he gives us privacy." We both sat on a sofa facing each other, and I handed Eva a glass of water from a tray I'd prepared before she arrived.

"And when you go to work, is he there too?" Then, a panicked expression crossed her face. "Are you still working?"

"I have a shoot tomorrow." My words eased the tension on Eva's face. "I'm not stopping no matter what anyone says." A prickle of irritation crept up the back of my mind as I remembered the way Damon told me I had to reschedule my shoot because it was inconvenient to his work schedule.

Asshole wasn't going to dictate my life.

He wanted to be with me at all times then he worked around me, not the other way around.

"Why is Damon telling you not to go to the shoot?"

"He has work commitments, and being at the shoot will cut into his day."

Eva took my hand in hers. "You can come stay with me if this isn't what you want. Lucian will back me up."

"I'm fine, Eva. I promise. This relationship thing is new to both of us. We're figuring it out."

"This isn't the first time he's lived with a lover." The intensity in her dark eyes told me all the things she didn't say.

She'd researched Damon's background or gotten the information from Lucian. She knew about Maria and bits and pieces of the rumors about him.

"I love him, Eva. And he loves me."

"I don't want him to hurt you and everything in me believes he's going to break your heart."

Her words felt as if she'd spoken an omen about my future.

"It's a risk I have to take."

That was when I saw Damon standing in the shadows of the hallway separating the living room and the front entrance. He held a duffel bag in one hand and his face and neck were covered in sweat.

What had my heart skipping a beat was the intense emotions in his deep emerald eyes, telling me heard the last part of the conversation with Eva.

All the spit in my throat dried up. The unexplainable draw for him compelled me to go to him. The need to touch him, feel his arms around me.

He moved forward and then nodded hello to Eva who seemed surprised to see him.

"How's the fitting going?" he asked.

"We haven't gotten to it yet. We were going to have some snacks first." I gestured to the coffee table with the spread of sandwiches, cookies, and pastries. "Want to join us?"

He shook his head, but that pulse of energy between us surged, making a tingle slide down my spine. "I just came to tell you that tomorrow when you go to your photoshoot, you will have a security team with you. They remain within eyesight at all times. No exceptions. Your safety comes first."

I nodded. "Okay."

"I'll meet you once I finish up with my meetings."

Of course he would.

I guessed I won some and I had lost some.

"Okay."

"Enjoy your snacks, ladies." Damon turned and headed down the hallway.

Once he was gone, Eva released an exaggerated breath. "Well then, I believe it's time to focus on my wedding gown. Your love life is something you'll figure out sooner or later."

"I'm not sure if that is a good or bad thing."

"Neither do I."

✧ ✧ ✧

"What's up with you checking your phone?" I asked Carla Justine as I came out of a fitting room and sat in the chair near the makeup artist's station.

From the moment I arrived an hour ago, all Carla had done was message back and forth with someone on her phone.

Regina Toro, a designer who we expected on set at any moment, despised anyone who used any form of electronics while on the clock. In her mind, if she was paying for our time, she wanted all of her attention.

She tended to be a hardass, but I got her point.

As one of the top designers in the world with celebrities, royals, billionaires, and the like begging for her to create custom pieces for them, she could do whatever the hell she wanted on set.

Thankfully, she liked me. However, her sense of humor was something I questioned. I glanced to my side and caught sight of an outfit resembling an old-school-style jailhouse uniform with stripes.

Hilarious, Regina.

"It's nothing. My mom is having issues with my sister. I'm playing interference." Carla tucked a loose strand of her blue-streaked hair behind her ear, glanced at the two female security personnel from the team Damon assigned to me, and tucked her mobile into the back pocket of her jeans.

"I'm usually the troublemaker fighting with my mom, so I'm no help to you. My older sister Eva gets to play your role."

I couldn't help but smile, thinking about how much I enjoyed my time with her yesterday.

Even if the conversation about our relationship was the last thing I wanted Damon to walk in upon, it had definitely worked out in my favor. He seemed to have loosened up about being up my ass at everything.

Now, I wouldn't jump ahead of myself and believe I had free rein to go any place I wanted, but work wise, Damon seemed to have accepted we both had demanding careers that required us to be apart.

The bodyguard situation wasn't new to me, so I could live with it. However, this crew was a hell of a lot more intense than the ones Lucian assigned to me.

"It's all good."

"What are they fighting over?"

"The usual."

"And that is?"

"Something you wouldn't have any notion about." She paused to open a giant box of cosmetics in every shade possible. "Money, of course."

"I can't disagree there. I grew up fortunate."

"I guess it helped to have your parent's money to get started in New York."

"I never took a dime from my parents after I left home at eighteen. They weren't happy about my choice of occupation. If you get what I'm saying."

It was more that they'd cut me off for being a disgrace, and the only way they would give me a dime was if I straightened up and came home to follow the rules they set under their roof.

"Seriously. How did you pay for anything? Was it a boyfriend or someone who set you up?"

"I had a little money saved up, and I roomed with a friend who had a studio apartment. But other than that, I lucked out and got a modeling gig almost immediately."

"Figures," she scoffed. "Your family name got you in the door."

I had no idea what was up with this chick. I'd worked with her on occasion, and she seemed nice enough at the time. Still, I'd never encountered these random digs at me about my financial status or connections before.

I heard her phone vibrate and then noticed her jaw clench.

Her attitude more than likely had to do with her family issues and not me. I'd let it go for now. I'd dealt with cattier situations than a makeup artist throwing snide comments my way.

"Because of my family, everyone knows me as Sophia Morelli, but professionally, I've always gone by Sophia Donatella. Look at the paperwork on the table."

Regina peeked at the docket with my name at the top and the list of outfits and looks for the shoot.

"Interesting. I never paid attention to it." A crease formed between her brow. "That makes no sense. Why wouldn't you use your connections to make things easier on you?"

"That's a story for another day. I will share that until my brothers decided to pop into a show and make my ties to them known, no one in the fashion industry knew I was a Morelli."

"All of your brothers showed up to a show?"

"Let me tell you, I was shocked, too. My brothers aren't discreet, and once you get a good look at all of us, the family resemblance is obvious."

"I can only imagine the spectacle they made." She fanned her face with her hand. "Your brothers have a scary reputation, but they're easy on the eyes."

I scrunched my nose. "If you say so."

"I do." She winked at me in the mirror. "Okay, I want to know one more thing before the squad invades. I hear them downstairs."

"Go ahead."

"Tell me about this man of yours everyone is talking about. I heard through the grapevine that he was the one that bought the million-dollar bikini you showcased at Karina's fashion show."

I knew Karina never divulged her client information, which meant she had a leak among her "trusted" staff.

"Where did you get that information?"

"So it's true."

"I've never seen it at his place, so I can't say so."

She wanted to dodge my question. I could do the same with hers.

"Well, that busted my bubble." She finished up my eye makeup and then focused on contouring my face. "So, is it true that he never leaves your side?"

Irritation prickled at the back of my mind. Thankfully, Damon bent in his need to attach himself to my side.

"You sure have a lot of gossip on me."

"Well, it isn't as if you haven't been the topic of news lately." She shrugged. "I'd rather keep our conversations lighthearted."

Fuck me. I'd rather be here in dead silence than chitchat with a gossip.

"Well?"

After Carla's last remark, she still expected me to answer, okay, I'd give her an answer. "He's not here, so that should tell you about listening to gossip. Don't do it."

"Oh, come on. Then is the security the reason he's not with you? He uses them to keep an eye on you?"

I shot her a glare. "I'm a Morelli. I've had at

least two people somewhere in the vicinity around me since I was born."

Technically that wasn't true, but this twat didn't need to know this information.

She opened her mouth to say something, then closed it as her cell rang with an incoming call. Instead of letting it go to voicemail, she stopped working on me to answer it.

Regina would lose her ever-loving mind when she arrived and saw that I wasn't ready for the first set.

And right on cue, a commotion of heavy footsteps followed by loud conversation filled the area behind us.

Regina and her staff of at least fifteen, maybe twenty people, came up the stairs. She barely had her foot on the landing before jumping into production mode. She pointed to areas around the room, giving directions and pointing at things on a tablet. Men and women dressed in clothes ranging from jeans and t-shirts to suits moved into production mode.

I shook my head, taking in Regina's outfit. How she could make a neon pink and blue sweatsuit and spiked green heels look perfect together, I'd never understand. The woman had this way of seeing trends and hitting the market before others.

A hunch told me, in addition to jailhouse stripes, neon was in my future.

As Regina continued talking, she looked in my direction. Her hazel eyes narrowed, and a frown touched her lips when she saw Carla on her phone. Then Regina leaned over to say something to her assistant, who nodded before approaching us.

I gave an internal prayer of thanks and then studied Carla's reflection in the mirror.

With any luck, this would be one of the rare occasions I'd ever have to work with her again.

It wasn't just her gossiping. Spreading hearsay was the norm in this industry, but something about her wasn't sitting well.

There was no easy banter with her. Most seasoned makeup artists perfected their chat game when they started their careers.

Then I found it strange she only knew me as Sophia Morelli.

People in the fashion world knew my professional name, especially those who worked with me. Only tabloids, gossip blogs, and non-fashion world media tagged me as a Morelli.

And what was up with her checking the phone nonstop?

Even the newbies in the industry understood to turn off their phones and focus on the job, and she seemed glued to it. And to have a designer catch you taking a call while on their dime meant no further jobs from them or anyone in their circle.

These types of things happened with models, too. Only the handful at the top got away with acting the fool. There was always someone younger, newer, prettier to replace you. It was the reason the industry was so damn cutthroat.

Regina's assistant, Vita, approached with a clipboard in one hand and a drink in the other. She had her blonde hair pulled back in a knot at the base of her neck and wore a casual green linen pantsuit paired with white sneakers.

Her smile was friendly, but her body language gave away her annoyance.

"Sophia, it is so good to see you." Vita leaned down to give me a double-cheeked kiss and then straightened, shooting Carla a death glare. "Fernando will be here in five minutes to finish styling you for the shoot. Carla is going home to continue her phone call."

Instead of commenting on what she'd said, I gestured with my chin to the designer convict jumpsuit. "So let me guess which outfit I will wear for the first set."

"It is Regina's way of commemorating the situation that caused us to reschedule for today." The sheepish grin on Vita's lips caused me to smile back at her.

"Regina is a menace."

"Oh, don't take it personally." Regina came up behind me, her black eyes alight with humor. "That pig is gone. Why not poke a little fun at your situation?"

"You're going to get me in trouble. I can see it."

"Sophia, dear. You aren't a murderer, even if you come from a family of mobsters."

"The proper term is a syndicate," Vita corrected, and I rolled my eyes.

"What?" I pretended to scoff offense. "You don't believe I could take Keith out? Everyone else thinks I did it."

"Everyone is stupid. If you did it, you would have cut his dick off and made him swallow it. Since there isn't a report about genital mutilation, I know it isn't you."

"Should I be concerned that you put such great thought into proving my innocence by thinking of how I would have tortured Keith?"

"Always worry about me. I'm a creative genius

who wants to stay on a schedule." She stepped back and clapped her hands. "Okay, everyone, we need to move. Let's get Sophia in her prison clothes."

I released a dramatic breath. This was going to be a long day. But at least I wasn't locked up in Damon's glass tower with him constantly watching me and nothing to do.

✧ ✧ ✧

SOPHIA, IT'S GO *time.*

My smart watch vibrated a little after one o'clock in the morning, signaling to leave Damon's penthouse. I'd spent too many weeks away from the women who depended on me.

A wave of guilt settled in my gut knowing I had to keep this from Damon. He'd eased up on his need to be at my side at every moment of every day. As long as my security stayed with me, he seemed to remain calm. Well for the most part.

Though it was still annoying to have him show up to a shoot without a heads up because he finished up work early.

This relationship thing was so complicated. Or maybe it was just being in a relationship with Damon.

Hopefully, I'd make it back here before Damon woke up for the day. I'd watched him set his alarm for eight since he planned to take the morning off and work from home.

Sliding from the bed in as smooth a way as possible so as not to disturb Damon, I tiptoed into the bathroom and then the closet. I changed into a pair of yoga pants and a sweatshirt and then, as quietly as possible, made my way to the front hallway.

Earlier in the evening, before Damon arrived home from work, I stashed my purse and shoes near the front stairwell.

Taking the stairs fifteen stories down to the floor leading to the gym elevators would suck ass. Still, it was better than the full thirty-five to go from Damon's penthouse to the ground floor. At least my ass would get in a good workout.

I was more worried about my return than anything.

Right now, the people milling about were at a minimum. However, when I returned, the employees of the various businesses that occupied the building started coming in, and most would recognize me.

If people weren't aware of me as Sophia Morelli, they knew I was the building owner, Damon Pierce's live-in girlfriend.

Once I reached the front entryway, I slipped on my sneakers and used the mirror against a nearby wall to set my wig on my head. There was no point in wearing contacts. They blurred my vision, and I needed to see my best for the work I had to complete tonight.

Picking up my shoulder bag, I slung it over my back and entered the stairwell, locking it behind me.

It's time to take care of people who need me more than I need an alibi.

Twenty minutes later, I stepped out into the crisp night air and strode toward the car waiting to take me to my destination.

When I slipped inside, the driver nodded his customary greeting whenever he picked me up for these visits and began our trek.

We rarely, if ever, spoke. He provided a service, just like I did. And the rules were, if we ever crossed paths in our real lives, we would act as if we never met before.

A wave of guilt hit me.

This wasn't how I wanted things with Damon. If he only knew how much I wanted to tell him all of it. Give him the details of what I was doing that night.

But the promises I'd made were things I

couldn't break, no matter how much they would help me.

By the time we reached a series of warehouses in an industrial area, I'd resigned myself to the fact that I'd have to continue to keep this from Damon.

I'd bear his wrath and whatever punishment he sent my way, and if it ultimately meant we separated, it was the price I'd pay.

The car pulled into a port, and I stepped out to find an older woman with golden brown skin and dark, soulful eyes waiting for me. She wore a long-sleeved black dress with a green apron covering the front.

Worry etched her face, and she wrung her hands as if she expected me to back out of coming.

Suzette Owusu wasn't a woman to ever give away any of her emotions, and seeing her in this state told me she'd kept an eye on all that had transpired in my life over the last few weeks.

"Suzette, I'm so happy to see you." I walked over to her and hugged her.

She wrapped her arms around me and then inspected my face. "Sophia, we are all so worried about you. None of us would have thought less of you if you decided to stay away."

I shook my head. "I don't break promises. The work you do is important."

"Because you protect us, the police arrested you."

"No, I don't ever want you to believe that. It has to do with things in no way linked to you."

"That isn't true. You were with us that night. If it means pulling the security tapes. I'll give them to you."

"Absolutely not. I will not put the safety of anyone here on the line. You've spent your whole life building this sanctuary. It has to remain that way."

Suzette used her retirement savings to create a safe haven for women and children seeking to escape abuse. She'd made a network through trusted people in the community, and they brought them to her.

I'd learned of her organization four years ago while helping at a women's outreach center during Christmas instead of spending it with Mom and Dad as they expected. One of the volunteers and I hit it off and then I mentioned wanting to use my sewing skills for a purpose greater than the fashion industry. The lady had smiled and the next thing I knew, I was having a coffee meeting with Suzette.

It took another month before Suzette trusted me enough to reveal any true details of her organization.

I could understand her caution, considering the volatility of the lives of the people she protected.

"In good conscience, I cannot let you go to jail for a murder you didn't commit." Suzette tucked a stray gray hair behind her ear with a shaky hand. "I won't lie and say it doesn't scare me to do it, but I will go public to prove your innocence if necessary."

"Please, no. Your work means life and death that is a million times more important than my freedom." I adjusted my bag on my shoulder and then tucked my arm into hers. "Let's go inside so I can get started."

"You're such a good girl, Sophia. Why do you let the world believe otherwise."

I swallowed the lump in my throat. "I don't want the reputation I have. It's that I stopped trying to change people's opinions about me. They're going to believe what they want to believe."

We entered a hallway leading to a large open communal space. Inside the room sat women and children clustered around multiple sets of tables and chairs, many mothers with arms wrapped around their sons and daughters, and others were groups of ladies just looking for escape.

Those who understood no harm would come to them under the walls of this building seemed relaxed and talked freely. Will others, who I assumed had just arrived, watched everyone with suspicion and uncertainty?

A fierce protectiveness always overwhelmed me whenever I came here.

The number of stories I'd listened to from so many who found safety under this roof showed me how truly fortunate I'd been my entire life.

Logically, I understood it didn't negate my trauma or suffering. However, I had means the people here couldn't fathom, which made all the difference in the world.

"Do you want me to go to my usual spot or do something else tonight?"

"No sewing machines tonight. We have a new volunteer. You can show her how to do basic stitching and taking measurements." Suzette shook her head.

"I'm not sure if that look means something good or bad. I'm leaning towards bad."

A hint of amusement lit her eyes. "She's not our usual type of volunteer, but considering where she started in life, I can understand her desire to help."

"Meaning she started down and out but made it big? Is it a celebrity?"

"More notorious." She smirked and then patted my arm. "But her heart is like yours."

"How did she find out about you?"

"It was more her husband. He knows about us and occasionally donates to our causes."

A thought crossed my mind, and I asked, "Would this person happen to be here because her husband wants her to like him again or something like that?"

"No, I do this for me," a Russian voice said behind me.

Then, a second later, Oliana Dominik came around the corner. To my surprise, she looked understated and ordinary, wearing yoga pants and a sweatshirt that looked remarkably like the ones I had on and with her blonde hair tied in a messy bun.

"No designer duds tonight?"

"No. I like the people here. They're important." She scanned me. "You look tired. Is it lack of sleep from too much fucking or worry?"

Suzette coughed. "Sophia, I see you two are old friends. I'll leave you to it."

Suzette hurried toward the kitchen, and I shot Oliana a scowl.

"You're a menace."

She shrugged. "Suzette has eight children. She knows how sex works."

"Okay, now I see why Nikki sent you here to volunteer. He thinks seeing a seventy-something-year-old who popped out kid after kid will influence you to give him more babies and not stab him in the junk with your earrings."

"I kissed it and made it better. Nikki isn't angry anymore." She winked at me.

"I hope you're keeping track of your birth control."

She rolled her eyes. "Doctor, give me the shot. No more babies means no more babies. Five is good."

I led her to the large storage room, stocking all the donated fabrics and clothes.

Once inside, I cocked a hand on my hip. "What do you want with me, and how the fuck did you find out about me coming here?"

"You're very smart. I knew I liked you." Oliana smiled in a catlike way and scooted onto a set of storage bins.

"I'm waiting."

"Remember when I told you what I did in my

home country and that my orders were to "take care" of my Nikki?" She air-quoted the, take care, part of her statement.

I nodded.

"Well, the occupation that sent me to him is why I looked you up."

Uneasiness skimmed along my skin.

"Okay. Go on."

"It isn't something a child dreams of becoming. I didn't pick that job. It was picked for me when I was eight years old."

I watched her, unsure whether to grab the door behind me and run for it or keep listening. "What does that have to do with me?"

"Don't look so scared, Sophia. I'm not here in that capacity. You're safe." She smirked.

"So, what's the point of your backstory?"

"You'll understand soon enough."

I watched her, still not sure if I could trust her.

"You had a role to fill in your family. It would have protected you and kept you safe in a little bubble. Why didn't you do it?"

"What does this have to do with anything?"

"I'm curious?"

"Because I'd rather pave my own path than be under anyone's thumb." I blew out a frustrated breath. "Seriously, Oliana, why are you stalking me? This is ridiculous."

She shrugged her shoulders. "It's simple. I like to know everything about people in the lives of my family."

"What family? I'm so lost right now."

Oliana crossed her arms. "Let me put it this way. Nobody touches my family and lives to tell the tail. Too bad someone got to him before I could."

Then it dawned on me what the hell she was talking about.

"You're related to Alice Stansbury. But her family comes from the Midwest, not Russia."

My heart ached as I remembered the devastation on poor sweet Alice's face after I found the young model curled into a ball in a bathroom stall after a fashion show. Keith Randolph had cornered the teen, assaulted her, and threatened to destroy her career if she told anyone about it.

That bastard had taken away a huge part of her bright eyed innocence and shattered so many of her dreams. That situation had been a major catalyst for my visit to the jackass's penthouse and the misfortune that took place to his new collection.

"As I said, I didn't have a choice for my job.

And neither did my sister." With her next words, Oliana's accent changed to pure American southern drawl. "We learn to blend in when necessary, especially when it means we can escape our pasts."

I couldn't help but gape at her. "You set that thing up in the precinct to gauge whether I killed Keith or not."

"Oh, I knew you couldn't have done it from the beginning. You Italians turn your nose up at the use of poison. In my book, if it gets the job done, who gives a shit."

"Yes, it is well documented how those in your homeland use poison to eliminate enemies."

"I prefer sharp objects."

"Considering you stabbed your husband, I would never have guessed. Okay, enough with the runaround. Come clean so I can get to work."

"You fascinate me, so I decided to snoop into your life. It is as simple as that. You didn't ask for anything from Ali, and don't use this place as your alibi."

"You have way too much time on your hands if you think watching the drama of my life unfold is interesting."

"You're innocent and want to save the world. I find it sweet."

"You are one of the strangest people I have ever met. Maybe you should have another kid, and then you'll be too busy to snoop in other people's lives."

"It wouldn't work. I can multitask. Here is some advice." Her face grew serious. "Tell your man everything. He won't betray your trust."

"How do you know that I haven't?"

"Lucky guess. Now, show me around."

CHAPTER FOURTEEN
Damon

"WHAT DO YOU mean no one spotted anyone with Sophia's description leave the building?" I clutched my phone to my ear, wanting to pull the idiot guard through the receiver and shake him. "Check all the feeds around the building and report back."

Hanging up, I paced my living room.

If I hadn't woken up from thirst a little past four thirty in the morning, I wouldn't have known Sophia wasn't in the penthouse.

I assumed she'd gotten up to grab something in the kitchen. Then, I quickly realized I was the only person in my apartment.

At first, worry coursed through me, but when I saw Sophia's purse and favorite sneakers missing, I knew she'd left of her own volition.

Where the fuck had she gone? And in the middle of the damn night?

What if something happened to her? The

killer was still at large and may decide to come after her. Couldn't she understand her safety was on the line?

She drove me near to insanity.

I ran a frustrated hand through my hair and then paused to look out the windows at the city and night sky.

She expected my unquestioning trust and then pulled shit like this. How the fuck was this ever going to work?

Was I doomed to impossible relationships?

I never lied about who I was or the capacity of what I could give to a woman.

Even knowing where I stood, Maria wanted things from me I couldn't give her, ultimately leading to her decision to take her own life.

It wasn't until Sophia that I knew any of the things Maria begged me for existed. The emotions, the desire, pushed at every part of my mind, leaving me helpless, overwhelmed, and definitely pissed off.

Maybe this was my punishment for not being what Maria needed.

No matter how much I wanted to shower Sophia with everything, she refused to budge an inch.

Perhaps this time, I was the one taking on

Maria's role. I wanted things Sophia couldn't give me, so she kept secrets from me.

Then again, she was a Morelli. Keeping secrets was something taught to them from birth. Lucian had a PhD in it, and from how things were looking, I'd say she wasn't far behind.

From my periphery, the bar came into view, reminding me of my childhood, and I couldn't help but snort.

I wasn't any better. Secrets were the Pierce family's lock and trade. Although we'd mastered securing every emotion under a wall of cool indifference and only allowing our moods to show through under the strictest circumstances.

When expressing feelings, the Morellis were a tsunami unleashing all its force on whatever object was in the way. Most people knew where they stood with the family. There was no hiding it.

We were also a product of our upbringing. For all of Bryant Morelli's faults, the one thing he wasn't known for was being a drunk. When it came to anger, rage, and abuse, he was a grand champion, just like my asshole father William Pierce.

However, William had one up on good old Bryant. Bill was a raging drunk. However, no one outside of the walls of the historic Pierce mansion would ever know it.

From an early age, I learned that tempering my mood kept the family monster away. My monster being my very own father.

William Pierce taught me more than enough lessons on protecting those weaker than me. He'd used his size, strength, and wealth to control my mother and sister. And it wasn't until an unfortunate incident that my siblings and I finally found ourselves rid of the bastard. But it wasn't until after we'd lost our mother under suspicious conditions. The fucker told us her health had failed, but I knew better, even if I couldn't prove otherwise.

That was more than likely where my drive to protect Sophia originated. Life's circumstances and my father's power prevented me from keeping my mother safe. I'd be damned if I let another woman I loved fall victim to the assholes of the world.

Except with Sophia, she refused to give one microscopic inch when it came to protecting her.

The irrational part of me wanted to lock her in this place, shackle her to my bed, and use every means in my arsenal to overwhelm her with sadistic pleasure to gain the information I wanted. She'd cry beautiful tears, come like a siren, and hate me in the end, but in the end, I'd be able to prove her innocence.

Clenching my teeth, I pushed those thoughts away. Losing her wasn't an option.

A creak sounded from the far end of the penthouse, and I immediately rushed in that direction. I should have guessed. She used the maintenance access and stairwell to make her way to the elevators near the health club.

As part of the building code, the city required multiple emergency exit points for my penthouse. The one leading to the fitness center happened to be one of them, and for security purposes, I keep it locked at all times. The only way to access it was with an electronic code or a physical key.

How the fuck could she have known about the stairwell, and who gave her the way in and out of it?

Well, I guessed I'd find out soon enough.

Deciding to leave the lights off, I propped a shoulder against the wall and waited for her to enter.

Not five minutes later, Sophia cracked open the door and tiptoed, shoeless, into the hallway. She wore the signature red wig she liked to don whenever going incognito. She carried her sneakers in one hand while the other held her favorite shoulder bag.

She set the items she carried on the floor, closed the door, and then pulled out a device from the side zipper pocket of her pants. She pressed it against a groove along the side of the keypad, and a second later, the locks on the door engaged.

"So that's how you circumvented my security."

Sophia froze, and a tremor shook her hand as she removed the object from the security panel.

"Mind if I have a look at that?"

"Yes. It belongs to a friend that will want it back."

"That's too bad." I stepped up behind her, crowding her against the door, and plucked it from her fingers before she realized what I had planned.

"Give it back to me. It isn't mine."

"What's the saying? Finders keepers." I leaned harder against her, sandwiching her between my body and the door.

"You didn't find anything," she gritted out. "You stole it."

"Wrong. I found it on you, and since you're mine, everything on you belongs to me."

"That logic is absurd."

"It seems I'm the furthest thing from logical

when it comes to you."

"Still not following."

"I'm not going to ask you where you went tonight."

"Why not?"

"Because I already know you won't tell me."

She dropped her forehead against the door. "I want to. You don't know how badly I want to."

"I didn't ask. Therefore, it doesn't matter, does it?"

"I'm sorry."

I pushed away from her. "Not good enough."

This woman drove me insane and nudged me to a limit that set me on the edge of being out of control. As her Dom, the last thing I could allow myself was to lose my discipline, my hold on the situation around us.

It was my responsibility to keep her safe, and she refused to let me do my job.

Maybe Lucian was right, I couldn't offer her what she needed, and I wasn't the right man for her. Nothing I seemed to do broke down the barrier between her secrets and me.

I picked up her things, turned, and headed toward the kitchen.

I'd barely taken a few steps when I heard her say.

"Punish me."

I paused for a moment.

She had no idea how I itched to delve out the consequences of her behavior. She deserved everything I gave her, and if I left her writhing, crying, and completely unsatisfied, it would have been all her own fault.

Instead of acknowledging her words, I continued on my path and set her items on the granite island.

Closing my eyes, I braced my hands on the counter's edge.

"Damon."

"Yes."

"Did you hear what I said?"

"I did."

"And?"

"And what, Sophia?"

"I want you to punish me."

I lifted my gaze to hers, and the arousal that seemed to spark to life no matter the situation between us ignited.

My cock hardened with the desire to redden her ass, watch those fat tears stream down her cheeks, and hear her scream her frustration when I refused to give her the relief she craved.

In the past, I wouldn't have denied a sub's

request for discipline. She wouldn't have had to ask. It was a given.

I couldn't think straight when it came to Sophia. I felt more, wanted more, needed more, and she sent my emotions into a tailspin.

Denial was the best option before I did something we both regretted.

"What form of punishment are you expecting from me?" I asked, resisting the urge to clench my fists. "I'm well versed in many methods."

She licked her lips. "I only know the ones you've taught me."

"Did you enjoy them?"

Her cheeks flushed, and she squirmed under my gaze. "At certain points, no, and at others, yes."

"This new lesson, you aren't going to like one bit."

Her brows furrowed, and she studied me as uncertainty and suspicion lit her dark eyes. "What are you going to do?"

"I'm going to deny your request."

"I don't understand."

"Punishment requires my attention. You don't deserve it. You haven't earned it."

"What the hell do you mean I haven't earned it."

"I'm your Dom, Sophia. The way a submissive behaves reflects on her Dom. All you've done is disrespect me. Once you've earned my time and attention, I'll give it to you."

"So you plan to punish me by ignoring me?"

I shook my head. "There is no ignoring you. I couldn't even if I tried. But I'm not going out of my way to cater to you either. You said you loved me, then decide if you can put me on your list of priorities."

"That isn't fair. I made promises. I can't break them. Don't you think I want to prove my innocence?"

"So my opinion on your innocence matters now? I thought you believed I questioned your involvement in Randolph's murder."

"I'm sorry."

"Not good enough." I pointed in the direction of our bedroom. "I suggest you go have a nap. You look exhausted from whatever you engaged in tonight, and I know you have a shoot later today."

"So that's it? You're letting it go. No forcing the issue of where I went tonight?"

What good would it do when I knew she wouldn't give me the answers to the questions I asked?

"You wanted punishment, Sophia. I'm giving

it to you. Until you accept what we are to each other, you don't deserve a moment of my time."

"Then I suppose you won't be here when I wake up?"

It killed me to be away from her. However, it was time to accept the more I caged her, the harder she'd fight to escape.

There was no winning for either of us.

I shook my head. "Probably not. I have some things to handle at the office and can only do so much work from home."

"I see." Her eyes glazed over with wetness, and then they cleared as she pulled back her emotions. "I've occupied too much of your time over the last few weeks. I apologize for bringing chaos into your life."

She grabbed her bag from the counter and angled her body toward the bedroom.

Oh, for fuck's sake. This conversation had gone to hell and back.

I stepped in her path. "That's not what I meant, and you know it. All I want is for you to share things with me."

"There is only one thing I haven't told you. You know everything else."

"It's one piece that will prove your innocence."

"To who? The authorities or you?" She pinched the bridge of her nose. "I believed you when you told me about Maria. I never doubted your truth even once. And even when rumors, speculations, and everyone around me tried to convince me to stay away from you, I accepted you as you were."

"Sophia."

She lifted a hand. "I'm not done. You admitted you loved me. From where I'm standing, your love is conditional."

"The hell it is," I challenged.

As if unfazed by my outrage, she continued, holding my angry gaze, "I'd rather live without love than have you place restrictions on it."

She pushed past me, leaving me alone in the kitchen.

CHAPTER FIFTEEN
Sophia

I LAY IN bed exhausted, unable to calm my mind enough to fall asleep. The scalding shower I took after leaving Damon had done little to alleviate the tension in my body. My mind and emotions couldn't uncoil themselves from all that transpired with Damon.

The want and desire were two constants whenever we were around each other. It was a visceral thing. This magnetic pull drew us together. At the same time, we were opposites who could repel wanting very different things.

How had we fallen in love? Was it even really love?

I knew what I felt. And it hurt to see that I likely wouldn't get what my older siblings had with their partners.

Damon and I had an intense passion, but it couldn't sustain a future together.

And was a future with him feasible?

Damon's possessiveness, need for control, and demands to know every bit of information about any situation overwhelmed me. And if I was honest with myself, it scared me too.

Those tendencies reminded me so much of Dad, and I wasn't sure I could handle a life like the one Mom lived.

In fact, I promised myself never to become a version of Sarah Morelli at any cost.

Dad had a control over her that I couldn't understand. An edge of menace laced all of their interactions. Sometimes, I wondered whether she liked it or accepted it as her lot in life.

One thing I knew for sure was that the violence between my parents wasn't something I'd ever endure. Damon punished me and left his marks on me, but they brought me pleasure. It gave me the heady feeling of bliss seeing the aftermath on my body.

It was the emotional roller coaster that I questioned.

Dad had destroyed something in Mom mentally. Now, she only considered her societal status and how her offspring represented her.

Was I ready for something like that to happen to me?

Maybe I was jumping ahead of myself. Until

we resolved this murder thing, I couldn't think of a future between Damon and me.

Rolling to my side, I gazed out the window to watch the sun cast its glow over the Manhattan skyline. This was a better view than the one from my apartment.

I wasn't sure how long I stared out the window when I felt the bed dip behind me, and then Damon's arm came around my waist to pull me close against him.

"Go to sleep. I'll be here when you wake up."

"But you said you were going in—"

"Shut up, Sophia. I'm telling you that I'll be here when you wake up."

"I truly don't know how to understand you. I may end up in an insane asylum."

"We'll be in there together." He kissed the back of my head and ordered, "No more talking. Time to sleep."

✧ ✧ ✧

"YOU WILL EARN your position as my wife, Sarah."

I cringed and tucked the cover on my bed tighter around me, hearing Father's sharp command.

Every single time they argued, it ended with them in the library.

Bad things happened in that room.

Father hurt Mom in there. He made her cry and scream. Sometimes, the sounds were so scary I had to put pillows over my head.

Why was my room next to the library?

I wished I was still at school, even if the ache in my tummy made me feel like I wanted to throw up. At least, then I wouldn't have to hear the fighting.

"Now, get on your knees."

"No, please."

"Do as I say, or you know what will happen."

"Don't make me do this. I'm begging you." *The fear in Mom's voice brought tears to my eyes.*

Oh God, what was Father going to make Mother do?

I couldn't stop shaking. He planned to hurt her again.

"You'll beg plenty by the time I finish with you. And it isn't as if you don't enjoy performing for me."

"That is different. Why did you invite him here? I don't understand."

Someone was in the house? But Mom and Father never entertained guests during the daytime.

"I have my reasons."

"I won't let you turn me into a whore."

Why would she say that?

I remembered Leo laughing with Lucian about him liking whores, but they didn't make it seem like that was a bad word. The way Mom said it, whore was a bad word.

"You don't get to tell me what I do and don't do." Father's tone grew harder, sending shivers all over my body. "I say I want to watch you suck another man's cock. You'll do it. If I say you have to fuck someone, you don't get to tell me no. By all that is holy, you are my whore."

"But you hate him. This is wrong. If anyone finds out."

"Since you can't take orders. We won't do it the easy way. Take off your clothes and get on the table."

I couldn't listen to it anymore. Why would he make her take her clothes off? He planned to hurt her and let someone watch. What could Mom have done so wrong that he would punish her like that?

A scream tore from her, followed by the sounds of clothes ripping. Then came sobs.

I scrambled from the bed, finding my slippers and grabbing my robe. I ran to the furthest point in my closet and crouched down under my winter clothes.

No one would find me here. The noises couldn't reach me here.

I wrapped my arms around my legs and buried my face against my knees.

I wished Lucian or Leo were here. I wanted Eva here. They kept me safe. When they were around, I wasn't so scared.

One day, I'd protect Mom like Lucian did when he was home.

The echo of flesh on flesh vibrated through the wall my bedroom shared with the library, making me burrow deeper into the closet.

Maybe if I closed my eyes and pretended, I was back at the busy show with all those pretty dresses and music I went to with Mom and Eva, I wouldn't hear the noises anymore. I thought of the fancy gowns in bright colors and the shiny skirts.

One day, I wanted to wear that and walk around in pointy heels like the models. Mom said I'd break my ankles if I tried it, but I knew I could do it.

All of a sudden, I realized the noises were gone.

Had Father and Mom left?

I gingerly walked over to the sliding panel connecting my room to the library. Deep down inside, I knew I shouldn't push it to the side, but curiosity got the best of me.

Carefully, I unlatched the hook, keeping the panel closed, and, as quietly as possible, pushed it to the side.

What I saw wasn't anything I could understand.

Was this how Father punished Mom? Was this what she begged him not to do to her?

Father had Mother naked and pinned to the pool table in the center of the room. Her head hung off one side of the table as he pushed his penis in and out of her mouth. And then, another man stood between Mom's legs with his back to me. He had one hand on her thigh and the other somewhere in front of him. He had his pants pushed down to his knees, and his hips shifted back and forth.

Father and the man stared at each other, not truly paying attention to Mom.

"Is this what you wanted?" Father asked the man.

"Not even close." The man said as he leaned down and bit down on Mom's breast as if he would tear it off.

She arched up and then cried out. Father never stopped pushing his penis into her mouth. It was like he wanted to choke her. Why would he do that? Couldn't he see that she was in pain?

The man then said, "Sarah, your pretty pussy comes so beautifully around my cock. I may have to make this a regular occurrence."

"You're a greedy asshole."

"So are you, Morelli."

"This was a one-time thing."

"You're the one who offered her up on the table. I plan to gorge. You're lucky it's your wife that I'm fucking and not one of your daughters."

❖ ❖ ❖

I GASPED AWAKE, trying to latch onto anything around me.

Damon grabbed hold of my roaming hands, setting them on his chest. "Sophia. I'm here. It was another nightmare. You're safe."

I clenched my eyes tight as comprehension seeped in. "Oh fuck. I remember. That night. What I saw. What they were doing. I remember. After all these years, why tonight?"

"What do you remember?"

Then I shook my head as nausea settled deep in my gut. "No, no, no. It was better when things were a jumbled mess in my head. Oh God. I'm going to be sick."

I jumped from the bed, rushed to the bathroom, and headed straight for the toilet. I barely opened the lid in time before my stomach emptied in what seemed like a never-ending rush.

"I've got you." Damon held my waist as my body continued to dry heave.

Once everything purged out of me, I dropped my head against Damon's chest and wept. All these years, they preached to me about virtue, conduct, and doing right, and they were no better than anyone else.

When the tears finally dried up, I looked at Damon and said, "My first sexual experience wasn't with me as a participant but as a voyeur while my father forced my mother into a threesome as a payment for a debt."

"Let's get off the bathroom floor, freshen you up, and tell me what you remember."

I nodded and let Damon tend to me. For fifteen minutes, he helped me wash my face, brush my teeth, and change into a fresh set of clothes. Then he led me to the living room and brought me a cup of herbal tea.

His domestic side seemed so different from the man he showed everyone. The world saw a cold, emotionless man, and here, or maybe with me, it was the complete opposite. He pulsed with every feeling under the sun, from psychotic obsession and possessiveness to sweet, tender caring.

"Why are you looking at me like that?"

"I'm trying to figure you out. You confuse me."

"I feel the same way about you, ninety-nine percent of the time." Damon sat beside me, placing my feet in his lap. "Tell me your story, Sophia."

"I was around eleven when my school sent me home for a high fever and a possible stomach bug." I recounted everything from the driver coming to get me to begging the teachers to let me stay since I hated being at home. Then I told him about the screaming and the yelling in the hallway and hearing Father drag Mom into the library.

As I conveyed the events of that day, the memory grew more vivid. I could recall everything from the color of my clothes to the smell of the air.

"I knew I should have turned around and run the moment I saw my mother's naked body, but I stayed and watched."

"In your other dreams, you never remembered what happened. Why do you think you remember now?"

"I don't know. Maybe all that is happening with the murder accusation, my parents, and us. I'm exhausted from holding everything in. My body wants to let everything go, and releasing these memories might be part of it."

"What was it that terrified you?"

"All of it. I was eleven. I knew nothing about sex. And seeing it from an extreme level like that made me fear it." I paused as a thought occurred to me. "What if that is the reason for my draw to kink?"

"Kink isn't about abuse, Sophia. Your father

abused his power over your mother."

"I know this, but from the viewpoint of a child. They wouldn't know anything about power dynamics, domination, control, and what was abuse or not."

"You believe your interest in kink stemmed from what you saw that night."

I nodded. "I watched my mother orgasm, not just once but multiple times, from a man my father gave her to. At the time, I couldn't understand what was happening. I knew enough to figure out it hadn't started off consensual or ended that way."

"Who was the man?"

"I wish I knew. I never saw his face. If I heard his voice again, then I might be able to link him to that night. But I doubt it. The only thing I can remember about him is that he had a small birthmark on his upper right butt cheek."

"And these are also memories through the lens of a young child."

"Now that I remember that night, other memories are flooding in. And I know it wasn't the first time something like that happened. It's like I blocked it out all of these years."

"You watched them again?"

"No, I don't think so. But I'm positive there

were other times I heard similar things from the library. It happened late at night when Lizzy and I were supposed to be in bed." I set my mug on the coffee table as queasiness started to churn again in my belly. "I remember different men's voices and once a woman's. I never saw anyone. I was too scared to leave my room. But the time with the woman, Mom cried and shouted how much she hated her. Then, like always, the sounds of sex came not long after the arguments and fighting quieted."

"They had to know you could hear them. You slept in the room next to the one they used for their sexual escapades."

"I'd like to pretend they were oblivious, but..." I trailed off, dropping my head, not wanting to think about that aspect of my childhood. "There was this incident around the time I turned twelve. I've wondered about it for the longest time and couldn't wrap my mind around what led to the fight that happened. It was like a piece of my memory was missing. Now it all makes sense."

"Go on."

"It happened a few days before my birthday. Mom offered to move me into a bedroom closer to Eva's. She posed it as an early present, telling me I'd love it since it was much bigger than what I currently had and it was time for me to have a room befitting a teenager, not a small child. When I refused, she lost her shit. No, she'd done more than lost her shit. She exploded with a tirade on how I was ungrateful and couldn't understand my fortune to be in the Morelli family. Then she lectured me on my responsibility of doing as my parents told me."

"Did she force you to move?"

"Of course. Sarah Morelli always got her way."

"Let me guess, you found a way to retaliate."

I smirked. "Two days after moving into my new bedroom, we had our Sunday dinner where everyone, meaning all the siblings and Father and Mom, sat together for a meal after church. Before the chef came out with the main course, I stretched my arms above my head. I made a flippant comment about how nice it was to finally get a good night's sleep now that I no longer had to listen to Mom and Dad watch television at a loud volume at all hours of the night."

"I'm sure Lucian got a kick out of it."

"He laughed his ass off, along with Leo. Eva tried to hide her mortification with a napkin, and all the other siblings had no clue what I was talking about." A shiver coursed down my spine. "Father, on the other hand, looked ready to strangle me, and Mom had turned a deep shade of red."

"It blows my mind you carried the memory of embarrassing your parents in front of your siblings and didn't know what it was about until a little under an hour ago."

"Yeah, well. No one wants to have images of their mother deep-throating their father while another man fucks her. I'd take memory loss over having something like that live rent-free in the forefront of my mind."

"Point, well made, Ms. Morelli."

Deciding I'd had enough of the conversation, I climbed onto my knees and over Damon's thigh, straddling him. I set my palms on his shoulder and stared into his mesmerizing emerald eyes.

"Are you still mad at me? I just shared everything I could about my dreams and gave you information about my past."

"Will you promise to come clean sooner or later?"

"As soon as I know it doesn't endanger anyone, I will."

"Endanger?" Damon stiffened under me, and his face grew hard. "I need you to explain this right now."

I resisted the gut reaction to push back at his order and said, "I can't tell you."

"Of course, you can't." He clenched his jaw, but then his face softened. "All I want to do is protect you. Why can't you see this?"

"I do. I promise. What I'm doing isn't anything bad. It's actually good."

"Good when it comes to you is a matter of perspective, Sophia."

"True. But I need you to trust me on this."

He captured my face with his palms and drew me to his. His lip coasted over mine.

"I do trust you. And until we find the asshole determined to pin Randolph's murder on you, I can't let my guard down with your security."

"I'm not a bird you can cage. I'm not the woman who wants the life Maria expected from you. I prefer to make my own decisions."

His fingers tightened on my skin. "Then you need to remember, you chose me."

"It still doesn't mean I'm going to let you lock me away in this tower of yours. I enjoy a life outside of you and plan to continue to enjoy it."

"Not without me, you won't."

"Good luck with that, considering you have a billion-dollar enterprise you are neglecting."

"I will punish you if you don't take care of yourself."

"Oh, like when you told me I don't deserve your time or attention."

"I was wrong to say that." He released a deep sigh and dropped his forehead against mine, then after a moment, he said, "This is all new territory for me. I don't know how to handle you."

"That's the whole issue. I'm not something to handle. You can't manage me. I'm not an object you can put in a box."

"If anything happens to you, I will unleash holy hell worse than anything Lucian's twisted imagination could fathom."

"There you go again, going straight from unhinged to psychopath."

"I'm serious, Sophia. I've cleaned up for your brother for years, and only a select few know about it."

"I figured out you weren't a mild-mannered, famous architect with a tragic history with women when said brother warned me away from you."

"The brat always has to make an appearance somewhere in our conversation, doesn't she?"

"Of course, she does. Otherwise, I wouldn't be Sophia Morelli."

CHAPTER SIXTEEN

Damon

"DAMON PIERCE."

I looked up from a set of change orders submitted by the construction foreman on a midsize high-rise to find two men standing in the doorway of the office I was using for the day.

Everything about them said cops, from their posture to the way they scanned the room. They wore suits, not designer but well-fitted, telling me they were detectives.

From the sneer in the taller of the pair's brown eyes, it was obvious he thought coming here was a waste of his time, and he sat in the why bother conducting a solid investigation when the boss says to do otherwise camp.

And the fact they tracked me down in a random office on a project site instead of waiting to meet with me at my company headquarters or at home, meant they were here to fuck with me in some way.

"What can I do for you, detectives?" I asked, pushing back from my desk, and stood.

The one who disliked me spoke, "I'm Detective Stuart, and this is Detective Hatch. We are part of the team assigned to the Randolph case and have a few follow-up questions that need clarification."

Interesting that these two came instead of the cops who'd held me in that interrogation room and questioned me for hours. These assholes thought I wanted to cooperate with them after they used me to get to Sophia.

Fat fucking chance.

I gestured to the empty chairs near me. "I'm not sure how much help I can provide you, considering my girlfriend is accused of murder based on personal vendettas and circumstantial evidence."

Stuart narrowed his gaze. "I wouldn't throw around allegations against the department without proof if I were you."

"That's right, making claims without evidence is the DA's job. You're only here to gain answers to questions of no consequence."

He shifted as if to come toward me, but Hatch caught him by the shoulder and then spoke. "My partner and I would like to ask you a few clarifying questions, and then we will be out of your way."

"Go right ahead."

Hatch glanced at Stuart as if telling him to stay quiet.

They took their seats and I followed, carrying my chair behind my desk.

Hatch pulled out his phone and read something. "Before we begin, I'd like to know, where is Ms. Morelli? From all accounts, she is with you at all times."

"Your accounts are wrong."

In my mind's eye, I could see Sophia sitting in her chair with a glamour squad around her as she prepared for whatever designer booked her to showcase their clothes.

From what Sophia could disclose about today's booking, the shoot was very hush-hush. They insisted she sign a nondisclosure agreement and even sent a car to pick her up since the location was secret.

Every instinct in my body wanted to fight her about going to a place where I couldn't find her. Who gave a damn about this famous designer and their magic collection of clothes. Sophia's safety came first.

When I was about to cancel my plans for the

day and attach myself to her ass, she walked over, informed me I could track her phone, and kissed my cheek.

The minx let me stew the whole time she prepared to leave.

"Then where is she?" Stuart asked with more of a demand in his tone than necessary.

There was not a chance in hell I would trust them with this information.

"I know where she is. That is all that matters based on the terms of her bail."

As if seeing he wouldn't get anywhere with me, Hatch decided to get to the reason for the interruption to my day. "We're here today to ask you about an incident between you and the deceased Mr. Randolph."

"I'm listening."

"Is it true you had a physical altercation with him concerning a business matter?"

Who the fuck gave them this information?

"I'm confused. Am I a suspect once again in Randolph's murder?"

"We are just clearing up some information from a few leads that have come to light."

"I have never done business with a Randolph or ever plan to do business with any Randolph."

"So you didn't have an altercation with him?"

Stuart jumped in.

This dick sure enjoyed playing the bad cop routine.

"Since I have an airtight alibi, any interaction I've had with the deceased is of no consequence."

Stuart shifted forward again as if to intimidate me. "You didn't answer the question."

"No, I didn't."

"If the altercation wasn't about business, was it jealousy?" The snide smile on Stuart's face gave me the urge to punch him. "Were you retaliating for a relationship between Ms. Morelli and the deceased Mr. Randolph? It's well known you're very possessive of your lovers."

Lovers? He knew about my lovers, did he?

Well, why wouldn't he after Maria's brother accused me of killing her in the middle of a gala not so long ago?

"Sorry to disappoint you; I sleep next to the woman Randolph wanted and wouldn't give him the time of day. Why would I feel a kernel of jealousy toward him?"

"Then were you protecting her from him?" Stuart leaned back in his chair. "She did make some serious allegations against him a few years ago. There are rumors that you're a dangerous man."

So they'd done their research. I wouldn't have expected anything less.

"Are there? That's very interesting?"

"There are also rumors you were involved in Maria Williams's death."

"Was that a question or a statement?"

I noticed a look pass between Hatch and Stuart and realized this was all a game to them. They wanted to see my reaction to them. Hatch acted the calm, quiet one, while Stuart acted the dick. Well, fuck them. I could play their game.

"You don't seem phased by accusations made against you. What does Lucian Morelli think about your relationship with his sister? You aren't the ideal boyfriend, considering your past lover was found dead."

"I'll ask him when we meet for drinks in an hour." I leaned forward in the same way Stuart had done earlier. "I know what you are doing. It won't work."

Hatch asked, "What are we doing?"

"You're wasting my time and trying to find evidence to pin a crime on an innocent woman."

"Is any Morelli innocent?" Stuart smirked.

I shook my head. "That's like asking if all cops are on the take. I believe it's time for the two of you to do some real detective work and stop working off rumors. Watching TV shows isn't considered learning on the job." I held Stuart's gaze, letting my barbs rain down on him. "Perhaps shadowing some real detectives may be a better option for you."

He clenched his jaw, and I couldn't help the smug satisfaction I felt.

The dick shouldn't dish it out if he couldn't take it.

My phone beeped in my pocket, telling me it was three o'clock and time to hit the road to beat rush hour traffic.

I never thought I'd see the day when I'd thank God for an order from Lucian to meet.

And here I was, happy to leave these assholes for a lecture Lucian planned about something he wanted me to do or how I needed to fix this or that for Sophia.

"Gentlemen, it's time to cut this short. I have a meeting to attend. Next time you have questions, contact my attorney. He will set up an appointment where we can answer every question to your satisfaction."

Irritation flashed across Stuart's face, but I couldn't give two shits. I gave them more than the courtesy of my time.

When I rose to my feet and started to gather

my papers, the men took the hint and left without another word.

Fuckers.

I gripped the back of my neck. It wasn't just the Morellis the cops wanted to strike at by going after Sophia. I was on their list, too.

She was my weakness. The one person that meant more to me than anybody else.

Dammit.

I only added to her trouble instead of shielding her from it.

I grabbed my jacket from the back of my chair and exited through the office doors.

I had to think.

Was I a selfish bastard for wanting Sophia the way I did?

Halfway down the hall, I noticed a packed conference room with a group of people standing around a table, looking at something in front of them as they compared various pieces of tiles, fabrics, and papers.

Slowing to look closer, I jerked to a stop as a body slammed into me.

"I'm sorry. I wasn't watching—" The woman trailed off.

I narrowed my gaze as I recognized her.

Henrietta Stanford.

She wore a very conservative business suit, completely opposite in style to the high-fashion outfit she wore to the club.

"Damon, I'm surprised to see you here."

"Why is that? This is development under Pierce Construction."

"I assumed you would be with Sophia, considering you don't seem to leave her side, and she is doing a very high-profile photoshoot today."

"What would you know about her shoot?"

She pursed her lips. "I'm in the business. I have ways of knowing things happening in the industry."

"Then why are you here, working in your former capacity?"

"I never turn down loyal clients who request work from me." She lifted her chin as if I'd offended her, but I caught her glance at someone in the conference room and gave them some silent communication.

"Wouldn't being on Randolph Senior's payroll prevent you from pursuing other projects."

"I have no idea what you are talking about."

Of course, she hadn't a clue. Too bad, my private investigator understood the necessity of gathering every piece of information possible on a person via any means available.

And she'd discovered that Papa Randolph wanted a choke chain on everyone who worked with his son before his death.

The old man continued running the playbook he used when Keith Randolph engaged in his first assault. He bought people out.

In this case, it was to spin a story of an artist lost too early. The people who used to spend time with Keith Randolph now lived mortgage-, rent-, or debt-free for the tradeoff of spreading stories of his accolades.

"I thought you'd remember mentioning Randolph at the club. You defended him with a passion that went beyond acquaintances or business colleagues. And"—I paused—"you made a point to go after Sophia about hearsay. It seemed as if you had an agenda."

"I only stated rumors and wanted clarification."

"If that was how you gain clarification, I wonder how you spread gossip."

"I don't need to gossip when the truth is much easier to discuss."

I took a step in her direction. "What do you mean by that?"

"You can't be serious. Everyone knows the open secret about your precious Sophia Morelli."

Rage, unlike anything I'd ever felt, boiled up inside me. Instead of allowing it to show, I kept my face in its standard emotionless mask.

"Open secret? I believe I'm in the dark about many things."

She patted my arm in a gesture of sympathy and familiarity we had never had before. "Lovers shouldn't keep secrets from each other."

She couldn't honestly believe that I was gullible enough for this bullshit.

"Considering our age difference and that relationships like ours are new to her, there are bound to be bumps in the road. We'll work it out."

"Perhaps someone closer to your age wouldn't keep childish secrets." Her fingers caressed up my bicep.

Deciding to play her game, I allowed her to keep her hand where it was.

Although if Sophia saw her touch me, there wasn't a doubt in my mind she'd come over and grab her by the hair and yank a chunk out.

"I'll let you know if things don't work out. For now, why don't we go into the office I am using, and you can fill me in on this secret."

She glanced at the room with the group and then nodded. "Lead the way."

Once inside the office, I closed the door and leaned against it.

Henrietta went to the desk and hurried on top; I could only stare at her.

She braced her palms on the wood beneath her and tilted her chest as if she were offering me her breasts.

If I weren't so curious as to what she had to say, I would have told her to get the fuck lost.

This behavior seemed a bit over the top, even if her attraction was genuine.

"You were saying?" I probed, ignoring how she ran a fingertip down the open collar of her shirt and between her cleavage.

"Your precious Sophia Morelli is damaged goods."

A throbbing headache flared to life in the back of my head.

All the information she had about Sophia came from one fucking source.

Keith Randolph.

The fucker had used the exact phrase when he'd spoken to me. As far as I knew, no one else had ever described Sophia in that way.

What did she gain by spreading this narrative? My guess pointed to one very likely conclusion. She was neck deep in framing Sophia.

But why?

I stood, taking a step toward her. "Fill me in on what you mean. We aren't living in the Victorian era. Women are allowed to take lovers."

"Is it acceptable to use it as a means to further their careers?"

"I'm not following?"

"How do you think she became an elite model?" Henrietta shook her head and then gave a dramatic sigh. "She slept with all the top designers to walk the shows. She started with Keith, and then when he broke it off, she accused him of rape."

Everything inside me wanted to choke the life from the woman before me for uttering those lies. Randolph Senior buried Sophia's assault and harassment complaints, and then, ultimately, no one ever looked into them again until recently.

This was another incident where only Randolph could have given her the information.

"Why do you care what anyone thinks about Sophia?" I asked when I was within touching distance of Henrietta.

A flush crept over her cheeks, and she parted her legs as if expecting me to step between them. It disgusted me to know I in any way aroused this woman.

She was a predator who wanted to hurt Sophia.

"Women like her don't deserve men like you."

I set my hand on the desk, caging her with my arms, and leaned forward. "What do you mean men like me?"

"Men who pay attention and take care of their women. She'll use you and throw you away."

"Are you saying you are the type who would take care of someone like me?"

"Yes," she whispered, staring into my eyes.

"You're with Rico. Doesn't that mean anything to you? How does that make you any better than you accuse Sophia of being?"

"What we have is open. We are partners and best friends but can be with anyone we choose."

"And you chose me."

"Yes." She leaned toward me, aiming for my lips.

I clenched my jaw and grabbed her wrists, squeezing them tight. "That's too bad because someone else already chose me. Her name is Sophia Donatella Morelli."

"What are you doing?" Henrietta struggled in my hold, but I tightened my grip.

"I want the truth. What is the real reason you want everyone to hate Sophia?"

"I don't know what you're talking about." She pushed at me, and I released her. "Have you lost your mind?"

She jumped from the desk and ran behind it.

Her gaze went to the phone on a side table, but before she could run toward it, I asked, "What did Randolph have on you? Or let me rephrase. What did he do to you to want him dead?"

"W-what?" Her eyes filled with fear.

Bingo.

"Either you killed Randolph or are involved in his murder."

"That's absurd."

"Is it?" I pulled my phone out of my pocket and pulled up an email from my investigator. "Did you believe I wouldn't have you checked out after the shit you pulled with Sophia at the club?"

"I didn't do anything to Keith. It wasn't me."

"Was it Rico?"

Her lips trembled, but she kept her mouth shut.

"Does your lack of admission mean yes?"

"He has nothing to do with this. You keep him out of it. He wouldn't hurt a fly."

Well, she had one redeeming quality. Henrietta honestly loved Rico.

"Then admit you killed Randolph."

"You think everything is so simple." Anger flared all over her face. "Do you know what it is like to work your ass off and then have some rich prick, daddy's boy take credit for your work?"

"Let me guess. Everything in Randolph's new home, fashion, and textile line was your brainchild."

"The bastard even took my fabrics for his new collection and then had the nerve to say he created every part of it." She wiped an angry tear from her face. "I was so happy when someone ripped those pieces to shreds right before his show."

"You wanted him to think it was Sophia who broke into his place," I accused, taking a step in her direction. She pivoted, expecting me to lunge for her.

I had no plans to touch her. All I needed was to keep her talking, and she'd never ever fucking hurt my woman again. Although she might find herself in a precious situation in lockup one day.

"Are you kidding me? I didn't have to do anything. The self-centered idiot couldn't imagine one of those hookers he underpaid and treated like shit would retaliate." She shook her head. "Everything revolved around this fixation on

Sophia Morelli. The jackass would get a paper cut and say Sophia cursed him for fucking and rejecting her. I doubt he ever touched her, and she was the one who rejected him."

"Randolph's obsession with Sophia gave you the person to direct suspicion while you plotted his murder. Am I correct?"

"The number of people who wanted that piece of shit dead is too long to count. During Fashion Week alone, Keith made more enemies than most humans do in a lifetime. All the cops had to do was a proper investigation, and they'd have no choice but to throw out the evidence they had against Sophia as circumstantial."

Yeah, but the DA decided to pursue a personal vendetta.

"Except that wasn't what happened."

She shrugged. "Not my problem."

"I'm going to make sure it is. You're going to confess and give Sophia her freedom back."

Henrietta laughed. "I'm not confessing to anything. At this point, it is your word against mine. And with your history with women, who would believe you over me anyway."

"You don't know anything about my personal life."

"Your last girlfriend died under suspicious

circumstances, and people believe you killed her."

"That's a narrative you're spinning. Maria took her own life."

"Her brother doesn't believe it, and neither do half the members of that club you visit."

The hairs on the back of my neck prickled. Stuart and Hatch got their information from her. All the rumors, all the bullshit. She was their source. But how the fuck did she get the information?

"What do you know about my club? You aren't a member."

"They call you a murderer and believe you killed your lover."

"I don't give a shit what anyone thinks about me."

"You will when the cops find your precious Sophia dead, too. It's obvious to anyone who has seen you together that you're extremely possessive of her. What would you do if you learned she wasn't at a photoshoot but meeting a new lover?"

My blood chilled as I realized everything from this run-in with Henrietta to Sophia's secret photoshoot was a setup.

Henrietta was creating an airtight case to protect herself.

She may have found me attractive, but she

never truly wanted me. Every-fucking-thing was an act. And now Sophia was going to pay the price.

I was a curse to the only woman I had ever loved.

"I have a deal for you."

"This isn't a negotiation. I am protecting mine and Rico's futures."

"Nothing is protecting you from the recording I made on my phone of our conversation." I pulled my cell out from my pants pocket and then pushed it back in. "I have your confession. I'll erase it right before you and eliminate every trace of it on one condition."

"That is?"

"You stop whatever is about to happen to Sophia."

CHAPTER SEVENTEEN
Sophia

I EXITED THE car outside a two-story brick office building near a loading dock and studied the exterior.

This place was where Regina wanted me to meet her for her super secret photoshoot.

Okay.

She was a creative genius, so there wasn't any point in questioning her. And since I had signed a three-year contract as the face of her new cosmetic and swimwear line, I guessed it was my job to show up where she told me.

Even if this place was a bit sketchy. And where the hell were the rest of the people?

I'd expect at least two dozen cars parked around the area instead of only a handful.

A chill slid down my spine, and I fingered the phone in my hoodie pocket.

Maybe a quick call to Damon was in order. Then he'd know my location, and this sick feeling in my gut would ease.

I shook the thought away. What was wrong with me?

When had I become so soft?

If I made it through some of the unsavory photoshoot locations from my early years in the industry, I could suck it up and take a few pictures in this part of town.

Then again, I never arrived at those locations and felt I was the only one in the area.

I had to get it together.

All of this Keith murder shit was getting to me.

Would Suzette forgive me if I told Damon about the shelter and my work there? The stress of keeping the information from him didn't seem worth it.

I jumped at the sound of a car's engine backfiring, and every bit of my attention sharpened to my surroundings.

Squaring my shoulders, I followed the instructions on the paperwork couriered earlier in the morning.

I punched in the security code, opened the metal door, made my way to a second-floor landing, and found a back room. Inside sat six long padded tables with fabrics and patterns arranged across them in various stages of clothing formation.

This couldn't be Regina's studio.

As far as I knew, she owned a giant block in Manhattan where she created and stored all her designs and inventory. Plus, this place didn't have anywhere near the security level I'd expect from an over-the-top tech lover like Regina.

I trailed a hand over a few pieces of the fabric, tilting my head to the side to better look at one of the sketches on the table.

No, this could be right.

I remembered seeing this dress in Keith's apartment the night I went in with Lizzy.

Was this his secret studio?

A prickle of fear slid down my back. Had someone lured me here as payback for killing Keith?

I looked around, seeing the simplicity of the area, and pushed away the thought of this studio belonging to Keith.

That prick would never come to this part of town to work. Keith liked the pomp and circumstance of having his creative space where people could ooh and ahh over him.

Then, I noticed the designs on a board resting on a back table. They were detailed layouts and patterns for fabrics. Next to it were multiple swatches in primary colors with tags labeled as cotton, silk, polyester, wool, and linen.

Adjacent to the board was a large binder labeled Project HRK.

Opening the folder, I found three sections divided into sections with the names Keith, Henrietta, and Rico. It was filled with calendars and timelines of tasks, centering around the development and execution of two textile lines, one for the clothing industry and the other for home fashions.

"No fucking way." I couldn't help but gape when I spotted Carla's name written in every spot where it said assistant duties.

None of this made sense. Her name was on items long before Keith died. Then why was she working the shoot with Regina?

My stomach dropped as realization hit me. This was supposed to be another of Regina's shoots.

My hand shook as I stared at Henrietta's schedule for the last two months. Right there in black ink for the night of Keith's murder, it said.

Meeting at Keith's for dinner-discuss next steps.

"That bitch set me up," I muttered under my breath.

The hairs on my neck prickled, and my palms grew damp as I reached into my pocket. I had to call Dam—

I froze, seeing the silhouette of a woman in my peripheral vision.

My heartbeat accelerated, and genuine fear slid down my spine.

"I knew you'd arrive early," Carla said from behind me. "Then again, Sophia Morelli is never late to her assignments."

Before I could respond or move, she spoke again.

"Let me change that. Sophia Donatella. You don't use Morelli in your work."

Keeping my body still, I closed my fingers around the sewing scissors at my waist level.

At least one thing all designs had in common, we kept sharp as fuck objects lying around to cut random things during our creative process.

"You went through a lot of effort to get me here today. I bet it cost you a pretty penny." I stated as I shifted, nearly dropping the too big shears on the table before getting them tucked away in my hoodie pocket.

It's good that Lucian wasn't here to see me

look like a total amateur with that move. Technically, I was an amateur, but as a Morelli, we were born criminals or something like that.

"I have my reasons."

"Did you have reasons for framing me for murder, too?"

She scoffed. "That wasn't me. I have no idea who did it. Besides, I'm just the help. Keith would never let me within five feet of him unless it were to force me to suck his cock."

The venom in her words conveyed how much she hated him. Keith had been a predator who abused and manipulated women. Everything in me screamed that he'd hurt Carla at some point.

"What did he do to you? If you worked with him here. I know he did something."

"It—it doesn't matter. Even if I wished it hurt more, the bastard is dead." She moved closer, and I noticed the gun she held pointed straight at me.

"What do you want from me, Carla?"

"You're here to clean up loose ends."

"Who wants them cleaned up? Henrietta?"

"Of course she wants it. He stole her work. But she got her payday for everything she lost, so I don't understand why she keeps bitching."

"She isn't happy with her deal with Keith's father?"

"She wants her work back." Carla rolled her eyes. "I told her to cut her losses, but no. I have to do dirty work to get my money while she gets to sit in her high-rise and pretend to decorate."

"How much is Daddy Randolph paying you to kill me?"

"Why do you care?"

"Call it morbid curiosity. I'm not leaving here alive. So your secret is safe with me."

She shoved the barrel into my back and grabbed my forearm. "I'll have enough to set me up for life so I don't have to deal with the problems a rich girl like you has never had to endure."

She really hated people who came from my background. I couldn't blame her, even if I knew we weren't all the same. Having money made life easier in many ways that I'd taken for granted. I never had to worry about bills or buying food or a place to live.

Working in the shelter opened my eyes to so many things.

"You have to know, Randolph is using you and your circumstances to get what he wants. He isn't the honest type. If you aren't careful, he will stab you in the back just like Keith did to the people around him."

"It's a fifty percent up-front and fifty upon delivery deal. The up-front payment alone is more than I can make in fifteen years." Carla jerked me in the direction of a chair. "I have that money put away in a Swiss trust. I'm not a dumbass."

She was if she thought I'd easily sit down for her to tie me up.

Fuck that shit.

I'd give it to her that she had more body mass and weight compared to me, and if she trained in any self-defense, she'd ring my clock. However, something told me that playing supervillain and training to be one wasn't her regular MO.

"Don't you think someone will notice if I disappear?"

"They will assume your very jealous and possessive lover did it. He has a history of murder allegations. Adding you to the list will make it easy."

I jerked around to face her. "Are you out of your mind? Damon is at a new building project trying to get everything back on track since they are running behind schedule. Dozens of people are with him."

"Wrong. His meetings are over, and now, his car is outside this building. Mr. Randolph had an acquaintance procure his vehicle and bring it here."

"Why would you do that to an innocent man? He never did anything to you?"

"Better him than me. I did my research on him. He isn't a sweet guy like you're painting him. He has a reputation. Toxic men like him deserve what they get. Just like Keith."

"Don't you ever compare Damon to Keith. He is nothing like that man."

"You keep believing that, but he will tie the bow on top of this endeavor, and I will get to live my life."

Not if I had anything to do about it.

"Good luck with that life when Daddy Randolph finds out Henrietta poisoned his precious son, and you helped cover it up."

Carla's steps faltered. "You're making that up."

"Check that project timeline and everything on Henrietta's schedule for the days leading up to Randolph's murder and after. She's the person he had dinner with when he died."

She shook her head. "I don't believe you. That's a lie. I won't let you ruin my future so you can trick me and try to save your life."

Was she listening to herself? Of course, I'd use any means available to get out of this situation.

She pushed me again, and this time, I shoved back against her. "That schedule is a printout, meaning the original is on a server somewhere linked to a computer. Eventually, it will come out."

"I don't care. You'll be dead, and I'll have my money." She jammed the gun barrel harder into my back and then kicked the back of my knee.

Mind-numbing pain ratcheted into my leg, and I screamed, tumbling forward. "Are you crazy? Just put a bullet in me and get it over with."

"Are you that ready to die?" She grabbed my hair and dragged me forward.

This time, I pulled the scissors from my hoodie, literally shredding the material in the process.

I angled my body enough to move and jabbed the blade into Carla's arm, forcing her to drop her gun.

She cried out and stumbled back as blood ran down her arms. I held onto the handle of the shears and faced her, gasping in breaths and trying to scan the room. I had to get out of here.

Spotting the pistol, I lunged for it at the same time Carla did and managed to knock it away, but not before she shoulder-checked me. I collided with a set of wooden cabinets, hitting my head against them and causing a bunch of boxes to fall off the top and onto me.

Oh God. My skull felt as if it were exploding.

After a few seconds, the pain cleared enough for me to have the strength to move, and I managed to push everything off me. Rolling to the side, I coughed a few times and then blinked until I could see through the haze in my eyes.

My focus landed on the handle of the scissors next to me.

Oh, that bitch was so dead.

If the cops wanted to put me away for murder, I would commit an actual murder.

I'd start by poking her eyes out. Yeah, that's what I'd do. After that, I'd improvise. I was pretty sure it's how Lucian operated most of the time anyway.

I clenched the shears in one hand and pushed to my knees, then nearly collapsed again as agony radiated out from the spot where Carla kicked me.

"Oh God. That bitch."

After a few deep inhales, I clenched my teeth and managed to stand.

I turned to face Carla, ready for whatever she planned. I blinked a few times, not understanding what I was seeing.

There was no sign of her. I scanned the room,

my focus landing on the doorway. The gun Carla and I fought over lay discarded on the floor near a pool of blood. However, Carla was nowhere to be found.

"Are you fucking kidding me right now."

She left.

She motherfucking left in the middle of all of this. And she forgot to take her weapon.

I shook my head at this ridiculousness.

Jesus. Lucian was never going to let me live this one down. An idiot nearly murdered me.

God, I hoped she fell down the stairs or something. At least, I could say I sliced her up with killer scissors.

All of a sudden, a dizziness surged through me, followed by crippling exhaustion. My legs gave out, and I slid to the floor, managing to prop myself against my nemesis, the cabinets.

Damn, my head hurt.

This day sucked.

At least I had evidence to prove I wasn't Keith's killer, or maybe I had it. I wasn't sure. I really needed a nap.

I should call Damon before I go to sleep. That would be a good idea.

Sleep was good.

No, no, no. I'd hit my head. Head and sleep

are not good. Or was it the opposite?

Damn, it hurt too much to think.

"Sophia. Look at me."

Who's shouting at me?

I looked in the direction of the voice. Damon's blurry face came near mine.

"C-Carla. She ran away."

"I don't give a damn about her. It's you I care about."

"I hit my head. I'm sleepy."

"Sophia, open your eyes. I'm going to get you to the hospital."

"But Carla."

"Stop talking about her." Damon pulled apart my eyelids, and I wanted to swat his hand away, but I had no energy. "She's not going anywhere."

"Is she dead?"

"No, she's not—Sophia, stay awake. The paramedics are almost here."

Why couldn't I move my body? Man, everything hurt. Damn, I was tired.

"I'm taking a nap." I leaned into Damon as his arms came around me. "We can talk later. You like to talk too much."

"I don't understand what you're saying. Dammit, your head is bleeding. This is my fault. It was my job to keep you safe."

I was safe. What was he talking about?

Once I had a nap, everything would be just fine.

"Sophia, stay with me. You have to stay with me. Don't you fucking leave me."

CHAPTER EIGHTEEN

Damon

"STOP GIVING ME those looks. It's creeping me out." Sophia glared at me from the passenger seat of my car.

Tonight was Sophia's first evening out since her incident with the makeup artist, Carla Justine, which left her with a hospital stay and three weeks of recovery at home from a severe concussion. She was damn lucky that she hadn't experienced a brain bleed, considering the amount of equipment that fell on her from atop the cabinets.

"I want to make sure you're one hundred percent."

"Stop worrying. The doctors said three weeks of rest, and I gave you six for your peace of mind. It's time to believe me when I say I'm fine."

I focused back on the road, not wanting to truly remember how battered she'd looked in our bed that I'd been afraid to touch her.

I wanted to destroy Carla Justine for the pain

she caused Sophia, but Sophia wanted me to let it go. In her eyes, Carla was another of Keith's victims and needed a second chance at life. And since she agreed to cooperate with an investigation against Randolph Senior and his alleged illegal activities, I could put my need for retribution aside for now.

In the end, Carla luring Sophia to the workshop and revealing the binder with the schedules provided enough evidence for the investigators to clear Sophia's name and shift their focus to Henrietta Stanford.

No matter how much the DA or his judge pal wanted to continue the case against Sophia, they had no choice but to drop it when all signs pointed to Henrietta as the murderer. Credit card history showed a history of plant purchases used for softening textile fibers produced by indigenous tribes in South America, which also has a history of utilization as poison in tribal warfare.

I turned into the Violent Delights parking lot and pulled into my spot.

"Are you sure you still want to do this with me?"

She shifted to face me, a look in her dark gaze that had my cock twitching.

"Ask me that again, and I'll say no."

"Sophia."

"Damon."

"Give me a straight answer."

"You told me I chose you, and now I have to live with the consequences. Has that edict changed all of a sudden?"

Everything had changed, and she couldn't fucking see it.

"You always have a choice."

"What happened to never letting me go?"

The best thing for her was to walk away, to break things off, and give her the freedom to find someone better for her. But I was a fucking selfish bastard.

I leaned toward her, holding her stare. "Did I say I was letting you go?"

Immediately, her lips parted in that way that told me she felt the change in energy.

"You haven't touched me since before the incident."

"That's a lie. You came on my mouth last night."

"I'm talking about your cock."

"That's another lie. If I recall, your mouth was wrapped around my cock this morning."

"That was me touching you."

"Spell it out for me, Sophia. What is it you

want from us coming here tonight?"

"I want the man who overwhelmed me that first night we met, who didn't hold back. I want you to fuck me the way you did after you realized you were the only man to ever be inside me."

"You're playing a very dangerous game right now. I restrain myself because you needed to recover from an ordeal I caused."

A crease formed between her brows as her lips tightened. "You're not the one who gets to take all the credit for the drama. You need to divide it accurately among the participants."

"You are truly unlike any woman I have ever encountered."

"Thank you. I strive to be unique."

"You strive to defy me at every damn turn."

"I'm a brat. It's what I'm good at."

She was not going to let me win this one, no matter what I said to her.

"Well, brat. Let me show off the prize that I've claimed."

"Will you promise to punish me and fuck me with your penis if I defy you?"

I sighed and opened the door. "Let's go before I spank your ass and fuck you right here in the parking deck."

Five minutes later, with a hand on Sophia's

lower back, I guided her into the darkly lit interior of Violent Delights. The attendants waited for us with trays to select or bands designating our status in the club.

When Sophia slipped off her long coat, I could only stare at her.

Sheer gold material cascaded over her body. Underneath, she wore the sapphire and diamond lingerie set meant to showcase her incredible body and curves.

Her friend, Karina Mehta's creation, left nothing to the imagination and gave me visions of everything I planned to do with her once we were alone.

She grinned wickedly and said, "I found where you hid it and decided tonight was a great time to wear it."

"That was supposed to be for me only."

"It is for you only. Everyone seeing it will know you claimed the expensive ensemble and the wearer."

"Is that what you want? You want everyone to know that you're mine and belong to me?"

She set a hand on my chest. "I want you to know this. I want you to stop walking on eggshells around me. I'm not going to break."

"You nearly died."

"No, I had a concussion."

"It was grade three."

"It wasn't your fault."

"We will agree to disagree."

"Carla is off-limits. And so is Henrietta, at least until after her conviction." She narrowed her eyes. "I mean it. And I sent that message to Lucian, too. I know the two of you have a plan."

"I have no idea what you're talking about."

"Both of you are menaces to society."

"I thought he was unhinged, and I was a psychopath."

"Same thing."

I offered her my hand, and she tucked hers around my elbow.

Within seconds of us entering the main lounge of the club, various gazes turned in our direction.

I had no doubt the rumors about me would forever circulate. No matter what, Maria's death would haunt me and follow me wherever I went.

No one would convince me I had no part in the choices she'd made. I was responsible for her and missed the signs of her turn to the darkness.

With Sophia, my failure sat on a level incomparable to losing Maria. Maybe that made me a cruel bastard. If I'd lost Sophia, I wouldn't have survived it.

I should have fought her on going to the photoshoot without security. Hell, I should have gone with her. How stupid was I not to see all the pieces of the trap when they were laid out right before me?

"Stop with the brooding, or people will think you aren't into your bratty submissive."

My eyes locked with Sophia's dark, humor-filled ones. "According to you, I haven't gotten into you for over six weeks."

"Oh, the serious Mr. Pierce is trying to make jokes. What will the other Doms say when they see I've corrupted you?"

I captured her face in my hand, drawing her to me. Her pupils dilated almost immediately, and her breath became unsteady.

"Did you forget I don't care what others think of me?" I grazed my teeth over her lower lip, nipping it right before I pulled back. "Your opinion is the only one I take into consideration."

"Well, I'm of the opinion we should skip socializing and visit a playroom."

"Public or private?"

"You'd let others watch as you fucked me?"

"Not a chance. This outfit is as much of you as I can tolerate sharing with anyone. All views of your cunt are mine."

"Then I guess the answer is private."

I led her to the same room we used the first night we were together. And just like last time, she paused in front of the picture of a woman bound with her hands above her head. The riding crop between her breasts helped showcase the jeweled clamps on her nipples.

Knowing the photographer who'd taken that picture, I was positive the flush on the model was the aftermath of an authentic orgasm instead of a preconstructed pose.

"Is this what you want, My Sophia?" I traced a finger down her spine, and goose bumps pricked her skin.

"You told me I wasn't ready before. Am I ready now?"

I circled my hand around the front of her neck to cup her throat and tilt her chin.

"You're more than ready. When we go inside, you know what to do."

I opened the door without another word. Sophia slipped off her shoes, pulled her sheer dress from her shoulders, and removed her jeweled bra. Once she set everything on a bench, she moved to the very table where she'd given me her virginity.

Heat filled her onyx eyes as her nipple pebbled with anticipation.

I studied various riding crops from a cabinet on the wall, some harder on the skin than others based on their flexibility. I chose one designed to sting, to give a beautiful glow, but not break the skin.

Then, out of my pocket, I extracted two sapphire and diamond nipple clamps.

"Definitely a lucky coincidence you decided to wear that outfit tonight."

"Are you planning to photograph me as well, Mr. Pierce? I am a model, after all."

"No, as I said, this is for me only." I removed my shirt, set it over her discarded clothes, and then moved in her direction with slow, deliberate steps.

A light flush crept up her golden skin, and that primal call to fuck the hell out of her surged forward. She licked her lips, and my cock became a solid weight in my pants.

I'd wait to fuck her, wanting her to heal, knowing what I craved to do bordered on violent desire.

She had to know I planned to rut into her until I rendered her unconscious.

"Stop looking at me like that and do something."

"What is your safe word, Sophia?"

She hesitated and then said, "Marriage."

Emotions like I'd never felt burned through me. Was the hesitation because she no longer feared it or that she still feared it and thought I expected it of her?

I approached her, cupping her breasts and teasing her nipples. Her lips parted, and I seized her mouth, losing myself in her taste.

This woman meant everything to me, and I fucking didn't deserve her.

Her arms came around my neck, and she pressed herself to me. I pushed her back, shaking my head.

"I'm not letting you distract me." I showed her the clamps. "I think we need to accessorize."

She closed her eyes and let her face slack, waiting for the sting that preceded the pleasure.

Leaning forward, I laved and teased her sensitive nipple, making it hard and tight. Then, when she least expected it, I gave it a sharp pinch with my fingers before attaching the jeweled clamp.

Sophia gasped and cried out. Her nails dug into the skin of my forearm, causing a biting sting that had surely drawn blood.

I inspected my handy work and found myself

mesmerized by the goddess before me. It was as if she'd lost herself in the pleasure-filled pain, mouth parted, exhaling shallow pants, her golden skin flushed with arousal. The beautiful stones hung from the tip of her breast, swaying back and forth.

This was the image to capture in a picture for my eyes only.

By the time I repeated the process on the other side, the tiny mewled sounds she made had me wanting to change all of my plans and just watch her come as I worked my cock in and out of her.

"Damon, I need you."

"Soon. Right now, it's time for the kiss of the crop." Setting my hands over the diamond waistband of her thong, I turned her, letting her feel how much I wanted her. "Bend over and set your hands in the cuffs."

The second she followed my directions, she cried out as the weight of the clamps tugged down on her sensitive nipples.

"Please, just fuck me." She pushed back against me, her minuscule underwear doing nothing to hide her dripping pussy.

"You wanted this, Sophia. I'm giving it to you."

"I change my mind. I'm a woman. I'm allowed to change my mind."

"Not in this case." Shifting around her, I bound her wrists into the padded cuffs and ran my hand up and down her gorgeous plump ass.

Taking hold of her thong, I slid it down her legs, letting it pool at her feet. I wouldn't risk breaking a jewel on her skin and marring her body.

She truly was a wet dream come to life.

"Ready?"

"Yes." She nodded.

I started slow, first with light taps across her legs and working up to her back and shoulders. Then I increased the force creating a sexy as fuck glow on her skin.

Each strike had my dick growing harder and harder and precum leaking from the tip. It was a slow torture for both of us.

The harder my strikes, the more she moaned. Her pussy gushed with need and soaked down her inner thigh, and the desire to drink it up called to me nonstop.

"Do you have any idea how beautiful you are?"

"I'd be more beautiful if your cock was in me."

I scored long strokes down her back. "You have a one-track mind."

"It's your fault. You started my sexual journey in this very room."

"I did. Then I guess you're happy with your path so far."

"Everything but the murder wrap."

"You're free. That is all that matters."

"I'm free because I didn't do it. A victim of the victim got desperate and took matters into her own hands. Her tactic would be my way of handling things, but she had her reasons."

Her words brought all the anger and guilt of the last few weeks to the forefront of my mind. Suppose Sophia had never met me if I'd never entered her life. Would any of this have happened? I wouldn't have confronted Randolph or caused him to go after Sophia. I was the reason Sophia ended up on Henrietta's radar, and because of Henrietta, Carla nearly killed her.

The common denominator in all of this was me.

I wasn't good for Sophia. I'd seen it from the beginning, and no matter how hard I tried, I couldn't stay away. I was like my grandfather. Bad blood. Unfixable.

Dangerous.

Ultimately, she paid the price for my weakness.

Lucian was right. Everyone was right. I had to let her go.

It would destroy me to do it. But I had no choice.

She deserved better than me.

"Reasons or not, I'm glad you're free."

"Same."

I trailed the crop up and down her body in a hypnotic rhythm. Then began a series of biting hits meant to sting and push her to that edge.

Would she tell me to stop? Would she say the word to make me stop?

No fucking way.

She released a guttural moan as her body tensed and her back bowed. In the next second, an orgasm washed over her.

She gasped and rocked back and forth.

"Damon. Oh God. Damon."

Beautiful. I could watch her all day and night.

Now, it had to end. It was time to make a choice.

Guilt cascaded over me as I thought of what I would do next. I'd lose Lucian as a friend and almost brother, but if it meant Sophia stayed safe, so be it.

I continued to work her, helping her ride the high of her release.

"Do you want more?"

"Yes. Oh, yes."

We were past the point where she could safely take more. As her Dom, no matter what she said, it was my job to stop. Her skin was tender. I knew better, even if she enjoyed the pain.

Fuck what was wrong with me. I had to stop. I needed to stop.

"Say your safeword, Sophia."

She writhed into each blow of my hand. "Why? I want this."

"Just do it." Then, not meaning to, I gritted out the word, "Please."

CHAPTER NINETEEN
Sophia

MY MIND WHIRLED with pain and pleasure, every thought a jumbled mess.

"Sophia. Are you listening? Say your Goddamn safeword."

I turned my head over my shoulder, holding his dark green stare.

His mood since the incident with Carla. He'd withdrawn. He promised never to put me in the same category as Maria, and he lied.

Now Damon planned to break us.

Not now, not here. After everything we'd been through, he gave up out of guilt.

Anger boiled up inside me. He would not get anything he wanted from me.

Fuck him.

"No," I shouted. "I know what you are planning."

He stalked over to my side, bringing his face right up to mine. "I will continue until you can't handle the pain anymore."

"Then keep doing it. I can take whatever you give me."

He closed his eyes, telling me this was the last thing he wanted to do.

He never wanted to be cruel or hurt me. This was all to make it so I never came back.

He grabbed my head, holding his against mine. "Why won't you ever listen? Why won't you ever do as I tell you."

"Because I get off on defying you, jackass. Don't for one second believe what you're doing is for love."

He released me, stood, and moved behind me.

Then came a series of battering crop strikes along my thighs and calves that left me dizzy as the agony of them burned through every nerve in my body.

I refused to give him any reaction. I held in every whimper. The only sign of discomfort was my tears. Those I couldn't hide, no matter how hard I tried.

"More," I demanded through gritted teeth.

"Dammit, Sophia, you don't want me. This will end as soon as you say it."

"Liar. I know what you're doing. I know what you're planning."

"You don't know anything."

This time he struck my ass. I knew I couldn't handle it anymore. It was too much. Everything hurt. Why was he doing this to us?

"Say it, Sophia."

"You don't get to decide. You bastard. You don't get to decide we're over."

He got in my face again. "I decide. I'm your fucking Dom. Just use the fucking word."

I stared at him, my heart breaking into a thousand pieces. I couldn't stay with someone who didn't want me.

"Fine, you want to hear it. Marriage. I said it. Are you happy? Marriage. Marriage. Marriage. Let me go. I'm done."

He moved back around me and then peppered my backside. I knew this would happen. The strikes weren't hard, gentle compared to everything, but they broke the rules, broke everything we'd built, broke us.

He planned this. And now we'd gone past the point of no return.

At that moment, two men rushed into the room, jerking Damon away from me.

They shouted about safewords and membership.

Then, Clark Ventana, the club manager, was

in my face.

"Sophia. Look at me. Do you need a doctor?" He unfastened my cuffs and threw a blanket over me.

"No."

"Yes," Damon countered. "Make sure to get the clamps off her."

I turned and stared at Damon.

He broke my heart, destroyed my trust, and was still concerned about my well-being.

Fuck him. Fuck him for making me love him. Fuck him for taking my choices from me.

Pulling the blanket tighter around me, I moved to walk past him but paused when I neared.

"You told me the choice was always mine. You lied. You're a liar, Damon Pierce. And know this. I will hate you forever for doing this to us."

✧ ✧ ✧

"HE'S DEAD BY morning." Lucian paced his living room, anger blazed on his face, and all I could do was give him a blank stare.

No matter what I said, it was as if he only heard whatever he wanted to hear about my situation or my life.

"Nobody is dead. This is between Damon and

me. Stay out of it."

"You're my sister. I decide what will happen."

I glared at him. "I'm going back to my apartment. I'd rather be alone than deal with this."

"You're not going anywhere. That fucker abused you." He sat across from me, set his elbows on his knees, and leaned forward as if he could intimidate me with his scary presence.

"Stop saying that." I matched his stance, making him frown, and he sat back, pulling out his phone.

"I believe what Ventana said. Pierce broke every rule in the club."

"Why won't you listen to me? He did it on purpose. He wanted me to use my safeword, and I wouldn't."

"Then it's his responsibility to end the scene and walk away."

"I'm going home."

"Sit your ass down, Sophia."

"Stop treating me like a child. I'm not a damn child."

"Then stop acting like one."

"Listen up, Lucian. I have been through enough over the last few years to make me more than capable of making my own decisions. I don't care if you are my brother or the king of the fucking world. I don't answer to you or anyone. I will leave, and if you don't like it fuck off."

"Try leaving and see what happens."

"I knew I should have stepped in as soon as the arrest happened."

"You couldn't have helped. Damon was the one with the clout to get me out. Besides, he's the one I picked to be with."

"We are your family. Your loyalty is to us. Not Pierce."

Was he listening to himself right now? This was his best friend we were talking about. Well, ex-best friend.

"Great, now you're treating me like Father."

"Don't compare me to that asshole."

"Then don't act like him."

"Then stop defending Pierce."

I took a deep, steadying breath. "There is absolutely no point in talking to you. It's like trying to reason with a brick wall. I'm going to get something to eat before I throw something at you."

"Since you refused to let the doctor give you the results of your check-up from the club, she will be here in ten minutes. Eat fast."

"I'm not going to die," I growled. "I have a few bruises but nothing more. The extra tests were an overkill. Why the hell did I need a blood draw? You're ridiculous."

"It's better to overkill than under."

"I don't understand how Elaine tolerates staying married to your bossy ass. I bet you were insufferable during her pregnancies."

"I have other redeeming qualities."

"I doubt it." I left him to scroll his phone and took the hallway to the kitchen.

When I was just outside, I could hear Eva and Lizzy talking. They had a habit of enjoying quiet time away from everyone in the breakfast nook, chatting.

Eva called it her bonding time with the youngest in the family.

Moving into the archway, I realized they were discussing me. I should have expected it.

"You need to get Sophia to eat something."

"Don't you think I've tried? I can't force her to eat."

"Someone needs to do something. Sophia just sits there and glares at us like we're keeping her prisoner."

I shook my head. Quiet talker, Lizzy wasn't—more on the end of an elephant stomping around.

"She can't lose any more weight, or she won't fit into the clothes for her next shoot."

Hey, I was recovering from a concussion. Besides, I liked pasta. I'd gain it back faster than the designers liked soon enough.

"She looks fine. I only want her rested." Eva, the ever-peacemaker.

"The wedding is in two weeks. I hope she will recover from whatever happened today. She needs all the energy possible to deal with Mom."

"Knowing Sophia, she will return to her usual fighting spirit soon."

"Well, it won't happen if she doesn't eat."

I adored Lizzy and Eva, and their mother-hen routine brought with it a sense of comfort. But right now, all I felt was loneliness.

I want so desperately to share what happened with them. Well, maybe not Lizzy, since she was still young and naïve.

On the other hand, Eva had relationships but never the type of dynamic I'd shared with Damon.

The one time I mentioned visiting Lucian's club, I had her freaking out and worried out of her mind.

I was almost twenty-six years old, and no one in my family saw me as an adult who understood how to live my life or make my own decisions.

Yes, I'd fucked up a time or two, but I'd

grown, I'd learned. Hell, I'd come out with a successful career. Still, all the Morelli family saw was that rebellious, outspoken teenager who needed to be reined in and restricted.

The only person to ever treat me like an adult was the one man who'd shattered my heart by not trusting in himself.

He'd given me the power to feel confident in me, my sexuality, who I was as a woman. I had the freedom to be my bratty, defiant, out-of-the-box self. I wasn't alone, I was safe, I was loved.

I'd returned to my previous role, the black sheep, the outsider, the one nobody could figure out.

My lips trembled, and I leaned my head against the kitchen archway.

How could Damon do this to me?

How was I going to survive?

Why was I always the one left behind?

✧ ✧ ✧

Thank you for reading DEFY by Sienna Snow!

OWN is the breathtaking conclusion to the Violent Delights trilogy. One click now so you don't miss the breathtaking, dangerous conclusion to the Violent Delights trilogy.

Want more family stories in Midnight Dynasty? They're ready for you!

- The owner of Violent Delights, Lucian Morelli in HEARTLESS
- Sophia's older sister Eva Morelli in ONE FOR THE MONEY
- Her secret sister Lyriope in steamy wonderland in KING OF SPADES

And if you're looking for more super-spicy kink? Then you definitely want to meet the Morelli's archenemy Winston Constantine in his modern-day Cinderella story…

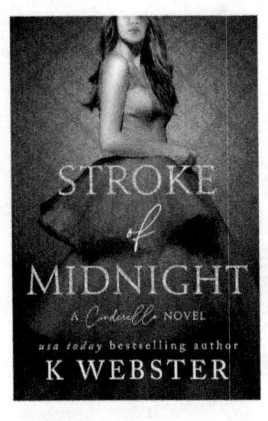

Money can buy anything. And anyone.

As the head of the Constantine family, I'm used to people bowing to my will. Cruel, rigid, unyielding—I'm all those things. When I discover the one woman who doesn't wither under my gaze, but instead smiles right back at me, I'm intrigued.

Ash Elliott needs cash, and I make her trade in crudeness and degradation for it. I crave her tears, her moans. I pay for each one. And every time, she comes back for more. When she challenges me with an offer of her own, I have to decide if I'm willing to give her far more than cold hard cash.

But love can have deadly consequences when it comes from a Constantine. At the stroke of midnight, that choice may be lost for both of us.

The warring Morelli and Constantine families have enough bad blood to fill an ocean, and there are told by your favorite dangerous romance authors. And you can get a FREE book when you signup for our newsletter. Find out when we have new books, sales, and get exclusive bonus scenes…
www.dangerouspress.com

About Dangerous Press

The warring Morelli and Constantine families have enough bad blood to fill an ocean, and their scorching hot stories will be told by your favorite dangerous romance authors.

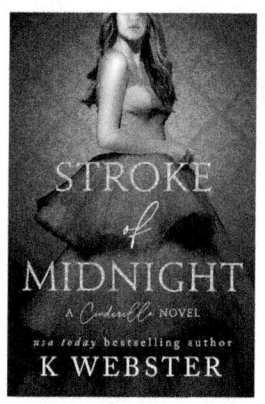

Meet Winston Constantine, the head of the Constantine family. He's used to people bowing to his will. Money can buy anything. And anyone. Including Ash Elliot, his new maid.

But love can have deadly consequences when it comes from a Constantine. At the stroke of midnight, that choice may be lost for both of them.

> "Brilliant storytelling packed with a powerful emotional punch, it's been years since I've been so invested in a book. Erotic romance at its finest!"
>
> – #1 New York Times bestselling author Rachel Van Dyken

"Stroke of Midnight is by far the hottest book I've read in a very long time! Winston Constantine is a dirty talking alpha who makes no apologies for going after what he wants."

– USA Today bestselling author Jenika Snow

Ready for more bad boys, more drama, and more heat? The Constantines have a resident fixer. The man they call when they need someone persuaded in a violent fashion. Ronan was danger and beauty, murder and mercy.

Outside a glittering party, I saw a man in the dark. I didn't know then that he was an assassin. A hit man. A mercenary. Ronan radiated danger and beauty. Mercy and mystery.

I wanted him, but I was already promised to another man. Ronan might be the one who murdered him. But two warring families want my blood. I don't know where to turn.

In a mad world of luxury and secrets, he's the only one I can trust.

"M. O'Keefe brings her A-game in this sexy, complicated romance where you're left questioning if everything you thought was true while dying to get your hands on the next book!"

– New York Times bestselling author K. Bromberg

"Powerful, sexy, and written like a dream, RUINED is the kind of book you wish you could read forever and ever. Ronan Byrne is my new romance addiction, and I'm already pining for more blue eyes and dirty deeds in the dark."

– USA Today Bestselling Author Sierra Simone

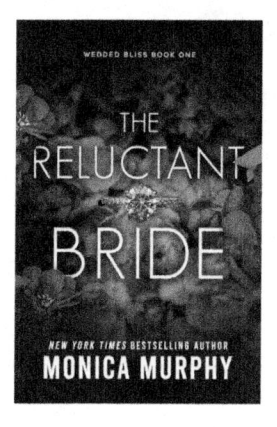

One moment I'm the forgotten daughter of one of the most wealthy families in the country, and the next I'm the blushing bride in an arranged marriage. My fate is sealed in my wedded union with a complete stranger.

"A fiery, slow burn that explodes with chemistry and achingly perfect tension. Monica Murphy has written a sizzling masterpiece."

– USA Today bestselling author Marni Mann

"Monica Murphy's The Reluctant Bride is a sinful yet sweet arranged marriage romance. I am in love with the Midnight Dynasty series!"

– USA Today Bestselling Author Natasha Knight

SIGN UP FOR THE NEWSLETTER
www.dangerouspress.com

JOIN THE FACEBOOK GROUP HERE
www.dangerouspress.com/facebook

FOLLOW US ON INSTAGRAM
www.instagram.com/dangerouspress

About the Author

USA Today Bestselling author Sienna Snow loves to serve up stories woven around confident and successful women who know what they want and how to get it, both in – and out – of the bedroom.

Her heroines are fresh, well-educated, and often find love and romance through atypical circumstances. Sienna treats her readers to enticing slices of hot romance infused with empowerment and indulgent satisfaction.

Sign up for her newsletter here: siennasnow.com/newsletter

Copyright

This is a work of fiction. Any resemblance to actual persons, living or dead, business establishments, events or locales is entirely coincidental. All rights reserved. Except for use in a review, the reproduction or use of this work in any part is forbidden without the express written permission of the author.

DEFY © 2023 by Sienna Snow
Print Edition

Printed in Dunstable, United Kingdom